DINNER WITH
THE DEAD

GAY BEAUMONT

FriesenPress

One Printers Way
Altona, MB R0G 0B0
Canada

www.friesenpress.com

ISBN
978-1-03-919962-0 (Hardcover)
978-1-03-919961-3 (Paperback)
978-1-03-919963-7 (eBook)

1. FICTION, GHOST

Distributed to the trade by The Ingram Book Company

DINNER WITH THE DEAD

TABLE OF CONTENTS

INTRODUCTION

A new occasion has been planned with guests from all areas of life, in regard to period and stages, death included. Interactions between the ages, political positions and occupational outlooks could become loudly petulant or blend with less aggression. Perhaps unbalanced, with a corset on one side and a cannon on the other. A 17th century powder puff and an early 19th century sawed off shotgun. One French and the other invented by Italian shepherds and brought to the Americas. Gangsters loved them. We'll thank the Italian shepherds for that invention, it was to ward off wolves. That's another word for thirsty gentlemen. Works well in a Speakeasy too. What combinations to have a martini with. How about at dinner with revolving tables? You are cordially invited to join this fusion of fun and risk. Gamble or play it safe? Let's crack one, $ $! And go for a cruise. Let's just pass by old Captain Bligh. Welcome to Dinner with the Dead, hold on to your head. Dress to distress. Champagne or moonshine, to your liking. Cheers let's celebrate the years!

Let's have a little history before we begin toasting each other. Long before the Mutiny on the Bounty which ended up not so bad with the Captain after thousands of miles reaching eastern Australia. Then it was known as the Dutch West Indies which is modern day Polynesia. Some men escaped there and were left. Several became dinner for the locals, others were poisoned by snakes. Those that got lucky, with natives that were friendly, were poisoned by sexually transmitted, very deadly disease. Great climate, shame about the races born there, reptiles or human... How about shark teeth being used as needles for an early form of tattoos, The ink from certain octopi would stain for the longest periods. While in India, bark from cinnamon trees were used with quills for needles, this giving skin decoration lasting eight to eighty days. The colors, darkness or lightness could be achieved by those more expert in this. To dye or not to die. Back to the Bounty, sailing endless kilometers to land, finding rations, and then continued on water again. After the mutiny eleven men were caught. The large ship sailed to England March 14, 1400 where the event was reported. In October 19 Bligh was acquitted of all transpired treatments and mutiny, then was promoted to Post Captain. Seven of the mutineers were hanged and four lived, interesting but only a short time before they met the same fate. A few great pub tales later...

Enjoy a voyage to the Caribbean once a year, winter most likely, perhaps this trip is a good one for you. Captain Morgan was knighted and went to Jamaica to become governor. Oh that demon rum... On these long voyages the men, needed to wash their tattered, filthy clothing. Using sea water they cleaned them as best they could. Hanging to dry inside the ship was too humid to evaporate, also fatal infestation of bugs to any dry food. Those that could stopped it once the doctor had figured it out. So now we hang what we have left outside. Having only bones of animals, fish and humans left to use as clothespins, the ship almost became a nudist colony. Yay, the wind took the rags away. That breeze feels good and dries the sweaty filth as well. Garments become scarce, but for a few young men whose fathers who were clothiers by trade. This new garment business was treacherous as sails were the only suitable fabric. Other than that the upper crewmen and captain who were outfitted in England with suitable or fine clothing, some even stylish. Stealing or using either sails or clothes of the upper crew were an easy death sentence.

Greetings to all and welcome to the intentional link of countless generations. I have sincerely tried to bring together individuals found in history from numerous eras, interests and life experiences. Personality and impulse we may find is the key to it all. I have designed a matchless weekend with guests of many backgrounds. Invitees arrive for cocktails at 5, allowing ample time to relax and reveal their past. Beverages built to liberate personality, then genuinely enjoy the friends and foe, as the clock chimes 8 times. Dressed in black, I'm a cool, cool cat that hates the cold unless in a glass. Clear liquid bubbles have yet to give trouble. Tonight's feast follows, offering choices from aimed influences. Appetizers through dessert, choice of dishes, I give you best wishes. Recipes designed for different times. A stretch for socializing afterwards before staying overnight. Our tomb service features breakfast as you wish. Invitations have gone to the deepest unfound tombs, underground to monuments and beyond. Most people with spirit have expressed desire to join, aiming to interact if possible. During this visit, who, and witch will show themselves and come? Nouveau encounters are granted this evening and on it goes. The gathering will give insight tonight. Your memory may be as misled as mine, I don't even remember having one. So let us talk as we lift a glass of wine.

As I am not yet among the dead, nor have any memory of dodging it. Although on one occasion I got close enough for many to believe I would never walk or talk again. Within a pulse of life, I was on hold for a long while. Not very elementary, my dear, thoughts will come. Existence can pick you up and just shake you. By the time you know it's hard to grow. My family and I were relocated while I was down for the count. I assume some felt the going could be good. What lay ahead of me was distorted, hard to believe life had hit this intersection. An accidental fall, down concrete stairs, left my brain hemorrhaging for some time before surgery. The only water in this fall was blood. I was disoriented and unaware of feelings. No recharging of routines to become organized. Life was dislocated like a 1000-piece puzzle recently opened and poured onto the table. Naturally I became reintroduced to consciousness and senses; to see, hear, smell and physically feel only. Life's lost and found; not necessarily emotion, and only some memories stayed. Love demise, a torn mind, and broken heart. Life was not kind, the first 2 decades gave struggle. I could not have tried harder to cross back. Accept me as your host, once close, but not yet a ghost. I have outlived most of my heritage. Surviving with unrivaled confusion, and neuro epilepsy.

Now therapy and exercise I have injected into my healing. This energizes me regularly without neglect. I've stepped out of the other stage I strayed in, almost ready after much delay. If our paths cross mark it with an Xcellent memory! We want to excavate information, and experience excitement to enjoy this excursion. New adventures unknown....

Permit me to introduce myself. My dub is Liza Gay de Saliva, born in Montreal, PQ, Canada, 1960. I have always been called Gay. Many people in my family were called their middle name, a tradition of south Asian sort. My father, Murray, born on the island of Ceylon, was named St Leger Hope Murray DeZylva. I'm sure he was not ecstatic about all of that, so Murray stuck. Uncle Imi Silverstone came to visit when I was born. My older sister was 3, quite busy, so Mom was too. He asked what I was called, and Mom had no answer. Imi said he would not leave until I had a name. After some time he said your first one is Kim. In Hebrew that means come... and Gay means go. Mom liked it, for both reasons, especially the typical joyful meaning.

I lived through an interesting time in history. Inventions, communications, travel off our planet and on, and computers. During which music, fashion, cars, social transportation and cities have changed and grown in massive proportions. From the ancient, vintage and recent to the mod. Hemlines went up as the music got down. People and thoughts grew faster. World wars, new countries, currencies and movements. Citizens crossed lands and oceans to join, creating new people and areas. Hope and help intertwined. I observed what I could in person and was able to read or watch history on film. Some re-enacted and much live, all interesting, easily absorbed. The Hospitality Industry is where I have worked most of my life. Many places and multiple positions have been my motto. From a nursing home to restaurants of many kinds and hotels across the continent. What hasn't come across the bill folder?

I came to find a great big development. It seemed there could be some uplifting propositions. An antique Inn with gardens on a speculative river went to auction... one, two, three counts, was mine! And so far, no vampires. Kind of like the stock market, there were many angles, no angels. Using everyone I could get my hands on, I played cat and mouse. The estate became an escape, a hole in the scenery. An upscale adult playground, worth many pounds. I gave it a nickname, The Inn and Out, but we were loved so much, the front was like a revolving door. Here I hope to hold a weekend party for a cross-section of people, a genuinely delicious and fascinating weekend event. Menaja mange. Please connect and appreciate what I have instore. Make your destination to my mature vacation mansion. As your host I will try to provide you with the most. If you like, we'll go slow, but get ready for the celebration station. Chug and choo

Does why have an answer, not to everything. Sometimes I feel a wave of drones and murmur. Who or what, I only know the impression perceived. It is like the imperfect purring of chords from a choir in the background, the hum of a beautiful song. It could simply be a universal rhythm, some sort of communication. Nuclear fusions where hydrogen converts to helium from explosions in the sun have existed since creation. Kaboom, we are a by-product of the big bang, a deep hum from the cataclysm. Was there smoke? Sounds like a great outdoor rock concert to me. My experiences come from the 20th and 21st centuries so I am not the earliest model. I have had doctors, many females with hormones on the left and small political pricks on the other. More have been sent this invitation so we may learn and be entertained by their history and escapades. With times long past, some millennials old, while others might be unheard stories told. For this occasion, there is an outdoor patio, lounge and dining hall. The Inn's suites are executive so there is quite a large space for the invited to enjoy. Our weekend time machine offers different levels, the Sea Section, the Fractured Rafters and the Chic Seats. Some might think it's not expensive, but life has been given to get them. Most guests are specters from former times, with their bodies, minds and history we dine. Time travel is the fourth dimension. Beside the general three we'll be using the fourth and fifth dimensions for this occasion, what a ride! It can't be only my choice, not to just survey the situations or watch, so let's get in there and dance with every dimension. Not only will the fifth take you to the other side, but it's also a great forty-five. To see and be close, as the specters arrive in the midafternoon sunlight, with slanting rays across the initial vision of their faces. I'd partake, and probably parlay. Pistols at 9 paces.

Time for another approach. Take pleasure in this new arrangement with a cocktail party and dinner with distinctive catering. Let's have a sip and take a trip. Included is a list of concoctions old and new, continental wines and many brews. Improvise at the restaurant, Carnivore Cafe, gamble with food but not the connoisseurs. If you should find a limb on the carving platter, keep your eyes on the company, table and your plate. Arsenic my dear? Perhaps plausible, but not necessary. Cuisine so delicious, almost a crime, food to die for. We could have the banquet buried but this is no funeral. The only cremation is the heating of Courvoisier. Most guests have whimsical interest and consent to interact, sharing incidents and their way of life. In existence there's some form of satire everywhere, even 6 feet under. From wherever you come may the twinkle of the midnight sky gleam like the setting of a summer sun. Most we have not forgotten, but from some, times of personal truth and memories may come out. Scandals narrating the joy of successful crimes, contributions to exploration and inventions, could be exposed and amusing. Perhaps plausible, but no necessity. Wicked but not wrong.

DEDICATION

For everyone living or dead who shares
my genes and my love, always.
.... And for the special ones who have been in them.
Life is live! Let's dance!

CHAPTER 1

MAINLINE

Let us launch relaxation while liberating stress and allow these words to flow. I'll inject the history and maybe a touch of mystery. Free yourself from any prejudice, presumptuous belief and partial impressions. Over endless centuries and a day, existence simple or complex, we can learn countless ways. A meeting can surprise and tease intellect, go ahead while you read, into a larger world. The exercise of life equates how long we keep our minds active. Allow this event to open your mind. After an initial deadly reception, meeting and relaxing, beverages are available in the lounge, our Spirits' bar. Dinner planned is set on a vast, circular table in the courtyard which will allow advantageous mingling. Tables in the lounge area are on the outer walls but do not worry about the vines near your wine. Dancing is a direct way to romancing, do you like older men? They've been around. The tables and sideboards provide resting places for befitting beverages, and any belongings during interrogation, a strong word for an exchange.

In this fashion one could leisurely stroll around, encouraging exposure to provide a surprising variety of company to encounter. Tonight, no fads, just comradery. Go with the flow and ease into the evening. Unlock any walls that block clarity and enjoy this event. Where will it take you? It is not expensive where you are going. Money and your past mean nothing, the heartbeat of lifestyle and experiences are the vault. In many minds the cost of ending seems great, but it will never be even with what you gave living. Each movement and achievement carried some failure and others triumph. They all cried out a unique story, personality or worldly destiny. Personal customs experienced their effects on life. This is the difference between imagination and being there. Make it as close as you can.

Let's go to a party, a mixed group of 300 to 3000. Whether belated or on time a celebration is no crime. If this is appealing let us pour a good portion to savor, in your honor a hearty, favorite flavor. Fabulous and expertly fabricated fermentation. A tempting sample to come into contact with. A mouth-watering three course fantasy. Formulated for you, feeling like warm skin on a satin mattress, starlight on one side and the barest of a breeze on the other. One leg bent at the knee in a downward position at leisure, covered by the thinnest weave, a silk strip just embracing the smooth curve. Slip a small sip, harmless heat. If you prefer shimmering bubbles which can spark your tongue, I suggest them both. For me a glass of robust red, as I've been completely bled. Costumes can be enchanting so perhaps rearrange historic dress. Please know you can come as you are, or for fun, not. Frankly, we may not be familiar with your time and culture. Simply create a comfortable cloak to socialize in for hours, unstoppable. For instance, John Wayne does not camouflage the deer thrown over his shoulder, dried blood from an arrow, but from whom and where, nobody knows. If his horse takes a spill, a solitary shot is no thrill! In acting, "break a leg" is only a wish of good luck. Jean Harlow brings the absolute best, simply a smile and a backless dress. Popeye has Olive Oil and spinach, that pumps him up, while Wimpy brings an IOU for a hamburger. Madame X would have you whip your own cream. WC Fields asks you to BYOB with just a little bit extra for him. Adam and Eve cannot spoil the soil, they come au natural in foliage.

A costume does not have to mask your face. One can dress festively in a dazzling disguise wearing specific make-up that both matches, then blends into the theme. No conspiracy of silence. Outfit yourself with the traditional clothing of the people and area, now overpowered. Obtain garments resembling an animal or object that have a characteristic of you. Or transport something that carries memories of your lifetime. Let your mind run free for inspiration. Something favorite that reassures and brings you recreation. Days clear or cloudy, dressing up or getting down, there are as many ways as possible.

Without containment when the seams split, I am a peacock, many shades from pink to blue. Natural or not I feel lovely when bringing them out, comfortable, cool and colorful. Feathers spread, energetic and alive with no dread. Believe me, I've tried, and succeeded on most occasions. But there were times I wasn't free to be all of me. I learned to close my feathers and hold. Having faculties, I grew to spontaneously touch people, without hands. Thinking about what I had, and gave, was special and appreciated. But when I had to shut it down, rest or change the scenery, I thought I would burst. So being colorful came with facial expression, words and an electric body. That is how I grew to express myself. No matter my appearance, those are my persuasive outer layers too.

Welcome to the Infinite Inn where you will sleep like the dead in our comfortable coffin-like beds, memory foam liners aid rest and recollection. We call these the cradle of life passed. Utilizing previously used boxes of primitive wood, bringing into play another's added spirit in guests. Join us anytime for a steaming cup of Columbian coffee, Free Trade… ha, who's kidding. Shipped here on our warm pavement, Route 666. Watch for those lifelike speed bumps, good, bad or different. Not the first or last underground railway, a universal mingling, first class all around. Tomb Service in the morning includes coffee or Ceylon tea, both shipped from abroad. Then you may choose Canadian peameal bacon and eggs with toast and juice. No need for Crossfit so how about a croissant? Fill out your desires on the form, sending telepathically or telegraphy, at your own risk. You may come back to life here so carry medication of choice or Viagra if you want to come back from the dead… 1800 and over. Throughout the years people shot game in the forest, a need. Here we can shoot the breeze anywhere with ease. Ashes come, some fiery and antique, don't look for vintage ashtrays. Here nothing triggers the dead so far. If you should lose your life halfway begin the games and let's play again.

The Inn can be compared to a large villa. There is the circular drive to the front door, an outdoor parking area on the east side and stables with carriage house on the left. At the front double door entrance is the main reception hall with a welcome area, registration and a large map of the facility. Access to the train is from the lobby. The Inn is stone and stucco from front to back. Guest wings, on both sides, are on the second and third floors. The main level has a large foyer, the bar, restaurant and gathering areas. In some places archways for easy passage. These overlook the vast garden squares with foliage and benches. No judges or politicians to worry about. See and smell the fragrance of the flowering trellises in an overhead curved fashion that complement the building. There are seasonal pools for swimming, fishponds and designated areas for warm weather sports. It sounds big and it is.

Henceforth is history, or is it hers? A vintage goblet of thin, pink depression glass, filled only with 1920 champagne, Louis Roderer or Veuve Clicquot. Cheers, no prohibition in sight! Let us take a flight to Florida for fresh oranges. A fresh cut, ½ orange squeezed, is juice with your champagne, a Mimosa. Options are cranberry or pure pomegranate juice, a deep dark fruit tase, almost pungent, but so good for anyone who has had their heart burned. Cheese and fruit will follow if chosen. Then freshen up at will, we may remember who you were. This evening is festive, if you feel free to costume, maybe dressed to kill. The day is yours to relax, have time to interact or run amuck. Happy hour begins at 4, starting our evening riot. Not to overthrow, a conquest to luxuriate and enjoy. Disguises tolerated as you may have an axe to grind. Some rumors lay as deep as the bottom of a grave. Guests may embellish fables or be creative in other ways. No borders, bring your own legend. The guest list from millenniums I have provided for contemplation. Many people from different areas of appeal and walks of life. Those that accept gathering for this engagement will benefit our interests. Will we see groupings or a tribal-like separation? Observing some invitees migrating, from one to another, enjoying diversity. It's not worth the cost, let any grudges be lost.

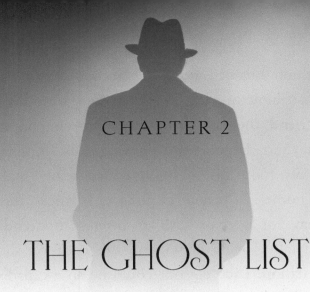

CHAPTER 2

THE GHOST LIST

Intuitive invitations sent, a cognitive announcement of intent, hopefully a temptation to join. Where to start? 4.1 billion years ago the oceans formed, 3.777 billion years until the first life was born. I remember them from high school. The recipients I thought of keeping to myself, as surprise has an advantage. Then the dinosaurs evolved, my first pair of leather shoes, followed by the Chixulub asteroid, hitting the earth 65 million years ago, crashing the party. After the slow creation of new life forms, past events resulted in unavoidable debt. What should they due? That time frame was the beginning of my hard to remember age. For an insatiable woman, hard is not something you pass by. Consequently the deciding factor will be past familiarity, and new desire. Will this, like a fish, be a lure to an unfamiliar situation? Would this succeed and the offer to attend a vintage style affair, with comrades through history, inspire presence? The strong belief in a first class gathering will bring some spirits high. No nonsense yet, or expense, moonshine is no longer fined. Notable memories, as clear as a still picture, bring validity. After your death, some family or friend, there's hope for a road carrying on, to a new form of beyond. Experience following these long deceased holds mystery. Inquisitive thoughts entice to solve and realize. Sherlock's home is a beneficial place to balance ideas. Some invitees may not agree or have less interest in attending this opportunity. But being present on this occasion should be a novel situation. Each episode could be an escapade. What endures, will it evolve? We will learn their illicit activities before death, even the cause of their last breath. The guests, not all dead yet, are offered a magic carpet ride for 10 sense. Happily ever after, is not necessarily comprehensive, but in our own way we journey life and death. Who can recognize if that road takes a wrong turn. However involved, regardless of actual or fictional, worthy sounds true. To the best of my deteriorating memory, not young but irrefutably youthful, the summoned are as follows. This is a lengthy list so relieve and, or refresh, at will. You could also add to your own history during this time and possibly be considered a beneficial climb. A deadly strike? Not here, living forever however you can.

Homo sapiens were the very first of us. 200,000 years ago in Africa, 100,000 years ago in SW Asia and 60,000 in the old world. Then homo habilis, the handyman with a larger brain case, the first maker of stone tools. My first husband was born to this useful tribe. During this neolithic period, neanderthal man with very long arms, lacking shoulder muscles, dragged his knuckles. Then the Foundation of the Egyptian State,

3050 BC. The first of ten dynasties, 2920- 2134 BC, began building in 2630 BC a series of private tombs. In 2660 BC was the initial construction of the step pyramid of Djoser. During this period emerges the famous history of Egypt, though its classical period was 3100 to 332 BCE. Preliterate symbol systems began establishing in the bronze age. Then society developed hieroglyphics, the first written language, around 3100 BC, at the onset of the phrenic period. Later on I surmise a piece of granite and a chisel produced the initial graffiti. One can garble on onyx marble… While alabaster added much beauty, it never meant to cause disaster. Their achievements have been exceptional both above and below the ground. These rustic graves, basically a dug cave, were the first fixer-uppers. The elementary tombs would evolve into academic and artisan crafted wonders in worship of the royalty. We will familiarize ourselves with the larger points of incest soon. Just a bit early for us to watch the family tree become an orchard, while more genealogy scientists' study. With interest let us start with Adam and Eve, their original jeans we have already seen.

Now a trip to Greece where everyone enjoys fine kalamata olives and wine, then be enlightened by the theoretical gents. Socrates, a scholar and teacher, was born June, 469 BCE, in Athens. His father, Sophrenisic a stone mason, and mother Phenorite a mid-wife. He likened himself to her practical duty. Bringing the truth of ultimate life, from deep within, needing help to reveal. Not a poor family but lacking noble birth. He laid the groundwork for the Socratic method of western philosophy. He had command over himself, controlling emotions and physical hardship, no pain is his gain. Almost unbelievable this desired trait, surely great discussions after eight! Political climate in Greece turned against him, Socrates was sentenced to death by hemlock poisoning in 399 BC. He accepted this rather than fleeing into exile. His theories influenced the viewpoints of Aristotle & Plato. These men's beliefs have come thousands of years, teaching great minds and society. Showing impressive, tolerant deliberation and ways to expand. Their love of wisdom, essentially an elevated value. Plato imparts abstract and utopian. While Aristotle tends to be more empirical, practical and common sensicle. If they were costumed, they would be original thoughts. Pages with the impressive markings of fundamental nature and wisdom, well read. Claudios Galenous, 129 to 199 AD, a known Greek Physician of importance. Discovering and naming arteries and their carrying of blood, yet not the circulation of it. The Galen theory was to determine a person's physical and mental qualities. Galen's humor of health regarded the four chief fluids of the body: blood, phlegm, black bile and choler. Add mental melancholy, pensive sadness. No man-eaters yet. In later life he became physician to the Roman emperor Marcus Aurelius. Other Roman history, unforgotten, finds interest with Julius Caesar. Always surrounded by senators. So, keep the knife if you should find it, it could come in handy.

In organized life the Egyptian society was structured like a pyramid. At the top were the gods Ra, the Sun god, Osiris and Isis, brother and sister. Osiris was both brother and husband of Isis. All believed in rulers of the universe. Then pharaohs entombed below, deemed divinity supported by servants and slaves. A long reign of relations including nineteen-year-old Tutankhamun, with his astoundingly luxurious tomb. Full of invaluable artifacts and his personal covering, forged into an impression of him. 200 pounds of solid gold, with traditional eye facial paint. His jeweled chest plate was an adornment made of gems and dyes. In power very young, surrounded by treasures, though not recognized as the god of the sun. Yet the brilliant paintings, and gold with precious stones were as illuminating. This amazing form, becoming traditional, was the use of makeup. Egyptians were not exempt to vanity. Physician Claudius Galanos extravagantly outlined eyes with coal, as it helped with the sun's glare. Rare realization, becoming stylish. Malachite for its green shimmer, when added made the eyes appear larger. Although personalized there is a similarity between Pharos. Hieroglyphs, their pictures on architecture and in tombs are authentic records of historical events. An ancient encyclopedia and photo album. The same elements of color were used for image representations, the addition of red came from iron oxide or Ceylon cinnamon bark. 1340 BC, a painted stucco coated limestone bust of Nefertiti, her beauty renowned. As royal wife of Pharoah Tuthmose the first, the sculpture included her flat crown. No suggestion she partook of vast glasses flowing with wine, regardless of her sensuous, slightly curved smile. The monumental pyramids and the Great Sphinx at Giza, all massive and astounding. One can go on with temples at Abu Simbel, The Valley of the Kings, then the complexes at Karnak and Luxor. These architects changed with the times, movement and different reigns. Outfitted with a set of workmen, non-union. Strike of disease unavoidable. Massive, awesome and magnificent representations. Skilled and accurate, still today. Shapes and measurements invented and used. Knowledge growing, forever showing. To this day the sands of time are still being removed to unearth more history. Skill and devotion bringing their life back to light.

Cleopatra, although born in Egypt, 69 BC, her family origins traced to Macedonian Greece and Claudius Ptolemy. Her beauty needed no makeup, but her conceit did. The benefits of Ptolemy's thinking contributed to mathematics, astronomy and geography. Musical theory and optics brought together bountiful and shrewd results. During this early history and period, with assistance she was well read, from a line of pharaohs typically inbred. Her natural parents were Ptolemy the 12th and Cleopatra the 5th, numbers an important archive. Travelling in any time, space or phase of life could ever influence or match the unique energy she had or propelled. At 18 she wed her brother Ptolemy the 13th, who was 11 years old. The honeymoon was a hysterical argument, never humorous, just angry. Typically, the bloodline was far too closely related. A wild roaring night with eventual blistering sex. Then, as mistress to Julius Caesar, she murdered her husband /brother, so their son could rule, Ptolemy the 15th, Caesar. These names, ongoing with numbers, continued giving history. Then, moving heaven and earth, the real deal. The historically famed romance with Marc Antony, a Roman

statesman, unmatched in battle and confidence. Julius
Caesar's right-hand man. Coming from parents Philippa
and Guillermo Munice, Greece and Italy joined to create
the unwavering Anthony. A mix of philosophy, geography,
romantic beauty and the seasoning of the Mediterranean.
Once in his lifetime he was captured for a desired ransom,
overheard with his natural vanity. During this entrapment
he informed the pirates his worth was much more than what
they had asked. Before Antony died in her arms from a self-
inflicted wound, he looked deeply into her eyes and told her,
"I know of nothing on this earth or in the heavens that could
kill this love". With large tears falling from her eyes she replied,
"When a heart is broken then a life is lost". Her faltering voice
trailed off. Femme fatale, Meow. Charismatic, intelligent and
ruthless in nature. Scratching several family members out to
become co-regent. One woman's legend, Cleopatra's life, legendary and full of wicked beauty. An ancient and fascinating
story of quality. Womanly prowess has many tales, some left
best unwagged. But for now, let's leave her asp alone.

Changing continents and millennia let us meet another
gentleman with brains and achievements, Benjamin Franklin.
As a leading figure of American history, he was a statesman,
author, mathematician and scientist. Whose inventions
include bifocals, a printer and a glass harmonica. A mature
man with a handsome head of long waving hair, with time
receding significantly. His fame and face are prominent but
let's not give him the brush off. Becoming a founding father,
helping to draft the Declaration of Independence, the US

Constitution and the peace treaty that ended the war. Abe Lincoln, 16th, President of the USA, in 1863 AD, made the Emancipation Proclamation, that forever freed the slaves after a bloody civil war. It also allowed them to vote. John Wilkes Booth said it was the last speech he'd ever make and shot him 3 days later in 1865. A barn Booth was in had been set to burn so he must exit. He was shot, his spinal cord was ruptured and passed. Avoid trespassing on your medulla spinalis.

Yet, in numerous places, to this day, people continue opposition. Despite years of seeing a variety of citizens belittled, and put in torturous situations, unchanged it remained. Why discard awareness and endure stupidity. They won't communicate and ascertain so there still exists the lack of sense and understanding. Despite years of reason and education, intelligence is hindered again. The presence of racism limits development and truth. Face the real world and work together. Blending gets better results, strength and human effort. Now enjoy complete variation. Back across the Atlantic in England let's go back a span in time. During the 6th century the knights of the roundtable, not a square in the bunch, protected King Arthur, the first knight among equals. Was he a myth or a reason. Chivalrous always, jousting for practice in the off seasons. Much later was Shakespeare's birth in April 1564. His written sonnets brought us his play Romeo and Juliet, teenagers hopelessly in love. Cheerfully exhilarated from friendship and profound passion, but each breath was plagued. Fear and probable death due to difference in family status hung overhead and between their shared skin. Already begun how could this absolute devotion adjourn. His plays were Tragedies with death and sadness. And Comedies, not continuously light, had happy endings. Histories were dramatizations of bygone monarchs and their distinction known in his time. In those days life was short. At 52 years old, in 1616, he had given every drop of himself. Wringing brains, sweat and tears on the feathers he inked. With bloodied fingers and chalices of wine, pages of wisdom, well red.

Brainstorming from scholarly to laboratory, in the sciences we hope to meet Marie Curie. Her discovery of radium and polonium were used in the procedure in treatments of cancer. Albert Einstein, born March 14th, 1879, in Germany became a theoretical physicist. He developed the theory of relativity in 1905. Winning the Nobel Prize, 1921, for physics and his explanations on photoelectric effect. While mechanically speaking, Henry Ford motored on the ground while the Wright brothers piloted the air. These fundamental men advanced the world with physical transportation, both on and off the road, no accident. A different kind of movement leads to Alexander Graham Bell, who studied sound waves. All due to his mother's deafness, his understanding of acoustics led to transmitting speech electronically. A constant pursuit, developing the telephone. With modern help is now worldwide and daily vital. Today portable cell phones have computer capabilities. Worldwide exploration involves bravehearted men. Christopher Columbus in sea vessels, Lawrence of Arabia on camel and Dr David Livingston in Africa. When travelling and at rest in tents, while getting loose, Lawrence relished playing dice. Taking pleasure in relaxation, enjoying this pastime. Was this the first crap shoot? Going on to the museum of Art we see the life blood of Michael Angelo and Leonardo Davinci who began the Mona Lisa in 1503. Vincent Van Gogh, Picasso and Degas also possessed this love. I will never forgive the thought that in modern day, these men could design tattoos beyond belief. Millenniums before the first tattooed man was 3370 BC. All working men either covered in paint, smudged with charcoal, or veiled by dust. Their minds and bodies suffered endlessly. Imagine jewelry designed by Van Cleef, Cartier, and Chanel, in museums, after being unearthed in Tiffany's tomb. Incomparable crafts. Not piercings for the body, those were originated by ancient colonies. If you are interested, 4000 years ago the first nose piercing was in the Middle East. In 2020 a man was discovered, with 12,000-year-old tongue and lip piercing, in Africa. Van Gough's depression on December 23, 1888 in Arles France brought mutilation. His self-portrait, 1889, the Bandaged Ear, showed the razor cut lower left ear he forced. Countless critical and laborious positions were an essential routine in the lives of painters. When inspired, the work was unsurpassed. Van Gough's The Potato Eaters, 1885, have not been invited to dinner. In the 20th century an individual, Andy Warhol, was an oil painter during the 60s. Interested in painting simple, singular pieces including a common pantry can and a Coca Cola bottle. In his studio most often, was his favorite drink, Coke. He was a fast-food fanatic enjoying Kellogg's cereals and Campbell's soup. So in the pantry his art subjects were loved and handy. He also painted popular famous people, uniquely accented scantily with primary colors. Charles Schultz was a cartoonist who read the funnies, comic strips in the newspaper every weekend. He loved B.C. and Lil Abner. Reading and watching these pieces closely gave him inspiration to draw. He is famous for his decades of writing the comic Peanuts, starring Charlie Brown, Lucy, Linus and Sally. Lucy with her psychiatric opinions, 5 cents, and her endless crush on Schroeder. Costumes are a part of our evening if you are interested. Speaking of attire...If life were fair, Elvis would still be alive today, and all the impersonators would be dead. Using your mind's eye is headquarters. From canvass or cardboard to cloth. From the 60s and 70s, the color practice on cloth, Tie Die, although long past its life, has no invitation for this weekend. But one never knows what tomorrow brings. Having a multitude of unique outlines and ideas, is my favorite designer, Edith Head. Her work was professional and classy, making many movies a standout. She was unmatched in 20th century costume design, and historical wardrobe, truly no disguise. Paris would never be embarrassed. Let's dress your house and home. With materials organic in nature, mixed with hard and modern, architect Frank Lloyd Wright was unparalleled. He bought pleasing efficiency. Configuring structures, unforgettable, no fraud. Functional, visually amazing and awed. Operation, no doctors required.

We have distinct moments of ideas and sight, not without days of despair. In the flash of life's creation, a surplus of energy from a group, or fireworks from a single person. A lack of magnetism can bring months of mediocrity, a prolonged pause. When someone says, "Let's get in the hay." I hope they are talking about bed and not a dinner. Turn a corner and be followed by the joy of change. Positive movement after a negative delay. The cache of sheer happiness, an inspiring caress. Age and maturity manufacture reality, a classic song sometimes sad, yet a compelling melody. If you are looking for something smooth, keep your eyes peeled, to avoid road bumps of any kind. Take a deep breath or two, and do not measure the pressure. In a short while, between periods of influence and impact, we will evolve between life and death. What a way to spend time between each heartbeat. Let us invite Beethoven, brilliant yet deaf, Mozart and Bach, such a symphony of men in the 1800s. For their time and type, talents unequalled, from keyboard to pipe. Listen more and tune in to these composers from centuries ago to enjoy their concerto. You would have to bend me dangerously to attend the opera. Tactless? … no glasses. An era, very special and important to me, from rhythm and sound it moves the very core of soul and body. Grounding. Forget the gravity and keep your spirit high. Keeping with music, from 1900 to today I am familiar with that progression. As times change, things loosen up a bit, with the freedom of charisma bringing unique talent. Tempo, attitude, instruments and compilation, never admit to misbehaving. Cole Porter, in 1927 starts to jazz it up. With intoxicating rhythm, activate good vibration and the cultivation of sound. Few factors remain the same,

Glen Miller, Louis Armstrong and Ella Fitzgerald. In 1946 Tony Bennet working in an Italian restaurant sang for the first time at 13 years old. In 1949 he had his first appearance in a nightclub. He attended the History of the Arts school, studying painting and music. His hard work delighted audiences, the cheers lift to cloud nine. He was still touring in the 21st century. Now change is the name. Rock and Roll and the Blues became the cues, so tap your shoes. Keeping time has lost all crime. During the nineteen 50s and 60s Frank Sinatra and Dean Martin crooned for us. It's the perfect time to take a breather, play the pack of rats and refresh your drink. Now some Ray Charles and Chuck Berry. Enjoy the encompassing music and splash the think tank. Rock on with Jerry Lee Lewis, then get stoned and roll with Mick Jagger and Keith Richards. Rod Stewart, Stevie Wonder, Bruce Springsteen, Steven Tyler, Elton John, and Eric Clapton. Some still making music, more than one way. Celebration of lifestyle, love ballads and events. Get slinky and sing a song of sex pants. This action has always been my passion. Blue Rodeo will ride endlessly. Many gone but not forgotten. Take notes.

Lend your hands on the dance floor. Waltzing in the 1830s, on your next turn lets learn the Charleston. Danced by flappers in 1923, faster moves of definition, change your clothes and mood. Their smile and fringe won't make you cringe. Improvising the jive in the 30s while swinging to jazz. Grow into the 40s and Mambo, 50s brought the Jive, cha- cha and boogie woogie. Hang on and twist into the 60s, 70s bump into disco and on it goes. Forward dance crazes and music took names and movements from some common items and songs. The swim, jerk, the mashed potato, shimmy, hitchhiker and the Watusi were popular in the late 50s and 60s. The 70s and early 80s were the disco and funk years, when inspiration was yourself and the hustle were suggestions to groove. Walk this way and get down tonight baby. From the act of sexual intercourse, slang brings the term come. In 1948, from a song Walking in a Meadow Green, launched by Billy Reid who found the loose folio. Who doesn't like a warm milkshake? Most music and songs were written from the heart, perhaps listened to from the backseat of a Chevrolet Bel Air convertible. Necking could lead to a hump in the road. Those potholes, the roller coaster of love. Beethoven or the Beach Boys, from a symphony to the sand. Or a dance craze, let's pick our fave!

Come and let us deeply take some air, stretch and bring in oxygen. You can keep stiff, but why not join the crowd? Healthy posture is advantageous, Alexander the Great's standby, whether reacting to, or proposing guests. You are the entertainment. Enjoyable interchanges our pursuit in the parlor. Regarding invitations in line of importance, imagine these people come often in strength. This may not be calculated chronologically. Let us bring a few greats that are a large part of ancient legends. Zeus, regarded as the center of thunder and lightning, rain and winds and his traditional weapon was a thunderbolt. He was called the father of both gods and men. Hercules, 1286 BC, a Roman and most powerful master, son of Jupiter Optimus Maximus, god of the sky and mortal Alkamine. He was also involved with Aphrodite, the goddess of beauty, brought forth from the waters of Paphos Cyprus. She had many gods admiring. Because of Zeus' ugliness she became the wife of Amphitryon. Watch out ladies, Zeus was a bit of a woman chaser. He tricked Hera into marrying him and continued a lifetime of infidelity. Such a snake, but what a way to go. Hercules had superhuman strength. Our muscular hero, so becoming, with lion skin nearby. Known to do things beyond any man or army. Millenniums later Sir Robert of Locksley from Yorkshire, in the early decades of 1300 AD, became the guise, Robin Hood. As a heroic outlaw he robbed the rich to give to the poor. His unmatched archery and swordsmanship helped his achievements and developed a growing group of followers. Bring your own longbow to Sherwood Forest in Nottingham. This man's real home is a castle, in a manor of speaking. These heroes, sometimes needing a darker side, come in countless forms.

From the trees to the seas meet some swashbucklers. Vice Admiral William Bligh FRS, officer of the Royal Navy, England. The mutiny on the HMS Bounty occurred during his command, in the South Pacific ocean, 1789. Set adrift in the ship's ocean launch, by mutineers led by Fletcher Christian. The admiral and his loyal men reached Timor-Leste, SE Asia, alive after 3618 nautical miles. After which he lived until 1817. The Earth is two thirds water, an ocean made for man with no gills. It stirs the heart, inspire the imagination and brings eternal joy to the soul. These words were felt by the Admirals while the exhaustion and lack of dietary needs consumed the sailors. True captain, James Cook FRS, 1728, Yorkshire, where

England's territory was fired upon with cannons and returned the same. His ship the Endeavor, sailed the pacific coast 3 times, trying to claim California, "Arcadia", for England. Looking for a passage around the North American continent he found the Bering Strait too tight to sail. Connecting the Arctic Ocean and the Bering Sea, named for Vitus Bering, Cook hoped to navigate a course to England. Ventures were numerous, both exploring new passages and wayfaring for wealth. When anchored his crew were adrift seeking more clues, artifacts and treasure. The first mate had a reputation of being a dirty dog. Don't leave your hand wandering on his wooden leg for a lengthy period, the gems there are only his. Still gambling for a staked prize. Upon their return Captain Cook had them searched for any valuables as part of his catch, what a stash. Closely inspected for articles of worth, gold, silver or jewels, if found went to his growing personal collection. With a sly smile he assured them of a fair share, like a french privateer. These vast vessels travelling with wind speed needed every available hand to man. The surrounding sound of flowing water and waves generally encouraged the urge to urinate. The sailors chiefly relieved themselves off the side of the boats, wind in their favor, they hope. These ships had very little convenience for the enlisted men, thank goodness for the poop deck! Ha, a more accurate description for these sailors is enslaved. Captain Cook was full of many things, including bile. Going past Japan around to Batavia, then Djakarta Indonesia, encountering malaria. The journey continued to tropical islands south, then New Zealand. Onward to the east coast of Australia which he claimed for England. His search for the fabled Antarctic continent, he landed in Tahiti, New Hebrides then New Caledonia. Years of sailing, learned with time, squalls and sweat. The crosswind over Cape Good Hope Africa, then up the Atlantic home. Decades of maneuvering challenges, work and adventure. Surrounded by whitecaps these captains set sail in British warships pursuing the unknown. Searching the seas for land, looking for treasure with hundreds of willing seamen to row and handle the ships. Travelling the briny depths brought new territories and invaluable prizes, they became known as pirates. In the distance an island, one with thousands of penguins, on the beach and in low grasses. The foothills rose to towering snow-capped rock mountains looking as if to hide piles of sparkling gems. The only plum jewels were the king penguins and sleepy seals. To the eyes alone, a flag ship, for buccaneers. In long seaworthy excursions of both hunger, thirst and disease, without land in sight. So fresh water, plants, fruit and any rest seem lost, except for the slightest blink of a memory. I would rather have the life and flesh eaten from my fingers, hands and body than have no relief. Take best care. Feeding, in all ways of life, is the most important respect for oneself. By your master and by yourself. Remember, three centuries ago, Lt. Robert Maynard sailed in the British royal navy on the HMS Bedford. He was a man of strength and dedication, seaworthy and straight forward. Yet how was he successful? In centuries past the recollections exist only in minds dead.

Famous of all these maritime men, Captain Edward Teach, known as Blackbeard, controlled the Caribbean Sea, from 1716 to 1718. He found a strong, local drink made of sugar cane and molasses, the darkish amber rum. He and some of his men enjoyed it often, cultivating relief and relaxation. He was known to raise a small beaker of imported West Indies' goods as often as desired. Or, if needed, for medicinal purpose. A form of this came from the Dutch west indies for hundred years earlier but that was another story with Captain Morgan. Remember that name the next time you go to the liquor store or bar. On Blackbeard's voyages, meat, grain and especially fresh water were needed. Heaven help you if you emptied a large wine skin of rum, into yourselves directly or to create a stash, for goods and services. When at sea remember not to sink the sip. To use one of these as a container for collecting fresh water, from a stream or pond inland could give you away. Be careful of what others might say. Their words of condemnation **at** sea, or on land, was the earliest marsh, a not so mellow roast. Making new skins from animals not a favorite task, but better than being a live shark snack! Taking the bladder, the largest, strongest and most flexible organ, so it holds more water than any other. After the animal or human was exterminated somehow the filleting and deconstruction of many parts would start. It was only the beginning. Above on the masts, hides drying and the organs flying came shortly after. The lads that made the clothes were organized to sew, tying the new skins and containers, then the collection of water began. In the meantime medium to large rats became roommates on board. There was not much to eat for anyone or anything, but they were the last game point. Well cooked, it's all good. Basted in rum, raise a glass.

Not the first shish kebabs. Cannibals used several lesser parts of seamen's bodies, no bones about it, including testicles. Whatever was easy to skewer with their smallest spears. Not the arrows, at times the points were soaked with life altering potions. Some caused death, others neurological damage, and specific ones triggered intolerable pain. Sharing is not always best. Once the kebabs were slowly cooked over the fire, what to use for dip? Why not the rum, discovered and distinguished by our captains of the seas. Travelling and landing in the tropical south, in several places and by many natives, doctors and drinkers alike, had discovered the production. Getting back to the trap the rat tails were used for many things. If left dry too long they would break, no dice. Hanging laundry, original twist-ties and decorative parts as fringe on the lieutenants uniform were some of the uses. Stuffed organs, octopi, birds and other edibles were delicacies, the fresh tails used to close them up in a woven style. How about just tie dyed... The stuffing could be the more delicious insects and snakes. Careful what you order tonight! Others, poisonous, were used as a death sentence. Sometimes you knew you were in for some form of punishment or death, but when and how was another mystery. It's already hot enough to sweat your guts out and that's only the start. Not time for attacking the heart. Some of these venoms caused excruciating torture, hours before you die. A few dried you out causing complete loss of all inner digested material, liquid or solid. Careful what you eat, you're going to see it again, and again, and you probably won't be the only man. Get out the popcorn, it's a double feature! Biting your nails is only an appetizer. Fingers in the mouth cover your handsomely beautiful face, which may give well needed relief. Just don't think of the taste.

As time goes on it chimes for the coming of something pleasing. We know of travel, whom, what and where. Learned from sincere needs a love for treasure of any kind. Landing again in a warm climate on a calm bay in the sun. Everyone takes a breath and a bath. The washed clothes are hung in the light breeze and the sailors, right up to the captain, are reasonably comfortable in the barely cool waters. Finally some smooth seas, sailors' rest, clean, naked and warm. Rum, exotic foods, fruit and their juices. Beverages of great taste and effect are concocted by our hard-working men. Drinking in balanced proportion relaxes, reduces tension and adds to the enjoyment of life. The moderation here is the addition of juices and any water. Native to this island, our Dutch west indies maiden, Om-yi-Ha, as she is called, her name is not forgotten. She shows a preparation of rum, squeezes of lemons, lime, pineapple and another juice of red sweet liquid. She puts it in an empty shell and shakes the life out of it. The shell had been placed in the cool, shady waters, along with a skin filled with other juices. Now the drink ends up in another tall glass shaped shell that has had water to cool it. That is poured out before the rum goes in, then refreshing shaken juices are added. The squeezing of the lemon and lime top this beverage off. She says Z-um-bye as she smiles passing you this. So thirst quenching, but the strength of the homemade liquor takes your breath away. The first lesson of drinking slowly. One, to enjoy awake, the other, to function. No Zombie outside the glass, don't be a foolish...

She is a beautiful bronze woman with a colorful fabric tied around her hips. A few flowers adorn her head of shoulder length hair. After a few sips you feel a strong swelling passion. There are others happily waiting for their gift, a cocktail. Don't split that word into two... yet. The captain comes shyly once the stars have lit the midnight blue sky. Om-yi-Ha takes the cold black coffee, some rum and a bit of sweet molasses. No cold shells, this at a moderate, mild temperature. This is shaken slightly then poured for his lord. Slow and low in the background some drumming starts, then a few musical notes plucked from a piece of split bamboo, come softly too. The full moon shone on Om-yi-Ha's hips as they swayed. Together the two moved, loosely yet close, as the stars glowed, and the music played. The night sheltered their glistening skin. In the morning she made us all a short drink of the slightly sweetened stronger coffee, the rum stirred slowly with a thin twig of bamboo. Good day, that will do! Memories of the evening stuck like glue. Small bites of food came in pairs or threes each few hours. Some vegetable crunch, some soft plants on a stick, lean, tender meat. Unknown but kind, slightly spicy, not sweet and juice filled fruit to finish. Fresh water available. To your health, men! A relaxing drink arrives as the sun started to turn peach, then a burnt reddish purple over the horizon. A calm ocean wrapped with trees. Life at its truest. A whiff of slowly cooking meat filled the air and these men were in another world. More maids arrived to serve on small, square wood plates each a portion of meat, plants and a small warm grain, like rice. The meat had been braised in a marinade, rum, a touch of molasses and a sprinkle of hot spice. Sliced fresh lemon and lime if you wished a squeeze. There is no comparison. Forgetting the months and years of hell, the frightening sights, the sickening swells, all the pain, tears of the fear of unknown, vanished tonight. Another drink, now stronger with both rum and coffee, a dash of white sinking to the bottom. A small purple flower floated in each short cup. A flickering fire glowed with crystal chunks thrown in. The maids motioned the men, a few taking an arm to follow. Into a warm pond they lay, with the candle-like fire on one side and the mysterious purple-amber sky above. Littered stars shone as silken skin slid along the men's firm, comforting arms. This was pure treasure, a charming pleasure. Thank you, Om-yi-Ha!

During the time of the 1880s there is a narrative of Peter Blood. In his British hometown he accomplished doctor skills and was known for this. The current ruler King James had no popularity, using commoners, taken as sea men to sailing ships, as well as rough tradesmen. Toiling was an understatement, drudgery and exertion. The men were given no pay, so this was slavery. There often was punishment, almost as entertainment. Yet how hard, and how long can a starving man work? Needing live bodies to help sail. Not haunting bold and hateful ghosts. Who's the blow-hard now? Here comes another hurricane. She, like all the others, have their own mind. The cities were an unorganized filth as the men rejected these treatments therefore causing the uprising against him. Nonconformist rebels, in agitated fashion, fought against this regime to the death. Unorganized groups, not large enough to go against the royal brigades, were committed to protest. During this campaign many men were left injured, dying and dead. One objector knew Dr Blood and went to his home in search of help. Afraid to join the men defying the King he was strongly hesitant. But knowing the men in this unconventional mutiny and their conditions, both his work and his heart merged to help. After time, most men perished and the last of the renegades were brought to trial. There was condemnation after one question, "Were you involved in this fight against the crown?" The word revolution was not used as there seemed no reason for any of these actions. Whether the men answered yes or no, many were sentenced to hanging. Left there until their shrunken skin separated at the neck and the bodies fell to the ground. The heads were left dangling for vultures, both flying and humans. During dinner, if having a salad choose the spring mix as opposed to literally sticking to the head lettuce. And, of course, dead men have long tales. Now comes hurricane of ravens, like a gorgeous flowing woman with spikes. Dinner here or take out. Most of the others taken aboard ships bound for the Caribbean Sea. Hundreds of men were bunked in hammocks, so many they were touching, swaying with the ocean water. These poor, hurt and hungry men had never been on a boat or sailed, so they learned as their stomachs churned. Binding ropes, swabbing decks, hoisting sails, searching the open water for other vessels, this rolling craft on undulating waters and hope became their daily routines. Beaten by angry officers from the highest to the lowest, the biggest and boldest. Imprisoned, not enlisted men tied between the tall wood, strapped with the hard, wide leather. A slashing smile from the unkempt merchant marines, drooling grease of their dinner, the abducted men would never see or smell. Eating only hard tack, biscuits made from flour, water and salt along with watered down stew. They drank rainwater caught in sheep's gut, together this was not enough to support the efforts for the hard, physical work. All unfamiliar and draining to their system, primarily unlivable. They were still alive, but barely. Sadistic conditions, this demanding work syphoned life. Ongoing objectional thoughts were constantly considered but scarcely whispered. When watched, the men ignored or slightly nodded to each other, knowing the strain but fearing all consequence. When there had been men's contemplation heard, Blood and others watched as the body was thrown overboard. Human seafood. The doctor had been given a stay from hanging and placed aboard a ship.

He was known to be looked up to by the others, so he was watched more than he knew. He tried to remain calm no matter the situation, but this new life full of action held no attraction. With sun singed skin, mucky foul tattered rags and inhumane treatment, his mind still worked. Always vowing to himself, helping others get better, to remember wellbeing and wealth. Anything but this. After landing in the south seas the men were auctioned off for pieces of eight to the seamen of the Royal Navy. Many went to plantation owners and a few to wealthy manors. Peter Blood was handsomely eyed by the niece of Colonel Bishop. The uncle was wary of having a filthy stranger in their home and shook his head. She looked at Blood closely and reminded her uncle with a pleading look. He found it hard to say no to her young, womanly face, so on the third try he agreed. They could have extra help on the grounds. So, from doctor to sailor, to tasks in a manor it was. Once he was cleaned and freshly clothed, they were amazed at his appearance and his speech. Having no idea, but a positive surprise, he was an educated man. Added was the care of the stables then as riding companion to the niece. Now she had her wish, sincere passion became her queenly fashion. He had nourishing food, water and some respect. Once they have more acquaintance it's learned he is a doctor. At this point it is hard to believe him as a common man. There had also been more news of the royal disputes in England to realize Blood's late positions. His vocation becomes called upon by the Governor, a gouty foot with constant pain and inflammation. It was to the point where he is unable to walk, and most concerned is the colonel. The climate helps but the injury incessantly offends. Life has more duty and interests, Dr Blood sees this as a benefit.

Most everyone remembers Christopher Columbus and his three ships, the Nina, The Pinta and the Santa Maria. In the last mentioned, Oct 12 1492 he discovered North America, landing at the Bahamas. The locals had another name, San Salvador, for it, but not long before it would change. After a long trip, the Spaniard himself enjoyed the climate and the rest. The ship, and it's mates were in total agreement. The long perilous trip, with spring and summer Atlantic Hurricanes, caused daily sickness and death from more causes. Most men were bruised on this cruise. The tallest reaching out to retract a boom, if you leaned your farthest, in a moment too soon, a shark, or other hungry sea animal would jump and have a bite. A tasty appetizer, then the entire mouthful, no matter how high the jump! The daily special. The acoustic crunching of the bones followed by the swish of flesh. Trips to the deck to slip or drop men into the cold sea were done during calmer times. Some of the rotting, aged dead below, were simply pushed through the closest porthole. When needed any hole would do if the body, wrapped in ragged cloth, arms rotted off, had become rancid. Once they had landed the fresh air and food were plentiful. Deep breaths and choices from the sea, land for meat, fruit and vegetation. A welcome mouthful, less decomposed, than any of the ship's remaining question-able food. Also aboard unplanned discoveries of men found, long deceased and decaying, in an obscure cubby or corner. Travels in the Caribbean, typically a smooth and enjoyable adventure, but on the Santa Maria in 1492, the ship ran aground in Haiti, and was abandoned. This crew was bruised and dashed on this endless cruise. The men had desperately picked usable lumber for dinghies, but only poor material found, so no good. This ship was an experienced traveler, and a well- built girl, yet her time had come. Nice name, now so many scraps, what a shame. They were rescued and returned in the Nina. With a smaller crew, so many typically died, of thirst, hunger and disease. As much food as they could carry was loaded for the departure. The question of supplies lasting longer than the first to be "shoved off", could be anyone's bet. No crewmember lives to leave any debts.

USA. Prohibition, no alcohol, nothing at all, for the general population. Wayne Weeler, leader of the anti-saloon league starts a protest. Getting to the supreme court, 1919. January seventeenth 1920 to December fifth, 1933. Days drier than the Sahara or a thirsty Captain Bligh before landing in Jamaica. But everyone wants to make a buck, not only North American accounts. Bonnie Parker and Clyde Champion Barrow robbed gas stations, it became natural. This was a convenient place, they often stopped to top up, on their escalating career. Their crimes quickly spiral from petty theft to bank robbery. Bonnie, being the most famous female racketeer, was originally married to Roy Thornton in 1929. Although she loved Clyde, she never divorced Roy, and died with her wedding ring on. And her colt detective special thirty-eight revolver was strapped to her thigh. The Prohibition brought a special brand of gangsters. Gambling and alcohol, girls and guns, big cars and fancy bars. All had to be hidden from the law. Clubs with misleading outer appearances concealed the action inside. Join these gentlemen for some American whiskey and gamble by shooting craps, cards if you prefer. Al

Capone and Johnny Torio had some mighty secrets hidden with smiles and big business. But they knew they'd be okay. Don't double cross the boss… Their dead competition would have on their stunned minds, the grass is always greener when you're above it. St Valentine's Day 1929, gang members dressed as policemen, heavily armed, went on patrol. Do not hang around any parking garage, Bugs Moran lost seven men, 2122 North Clark St. in Chicago, Thursday ten-thirty am. All callously shot standing against the wall. Ciao. Then gangsters John Dillinger and Baby Face Nelson left a trail of fear and protection. Nelson Became so treacherous Dillinger stopped working with him. In July 1934 John Dillinger paid for it during a confrontation with the FBI. A roaring time. Nelson killed the largest number of FBI members. Thank god I have done my duty were his last words, repeated until he could no longer speak, November 1934. The beginning of the end of the gangster era. don't double cross the boss. Add the tears of the moon to the drips of alcohol and the bounty. As for prohibition they turned stone to water, so to speak. We don't want to break your hearts, wait. Blood brothers can and will make wine. Spring, every time.

I weep for the happy, painless life I lost

Now less emotion, and moments free of agony

Life and its events came at too much a cost

Joyous once, then came pain, change can kill positive light

This teaches, gaining wisdom, then come some new questions

Time and words permit this writing, before another battle to fight

Are so many tears necessary, watering weeds, but drowning flowers

Natural to grow, getting older, true to life stories you have told

Remember a deliriously good start can turn into a savagely broken heart

Use it while and when you can, there may be changes to the plan

The end comes so fast, with deadly strength it lasts

The next fine group have spent lifetimes portraying people and events both true to life and fictional. On the big screen they have charisma and character. Rudolph Valentino, a lone wolf with upward aspiration and a large dedication. Boris Karloff, usually a sinister character, was often in the background with a perilous intent. Think of his only incident where his face slips, the decomposing of his head. Juicy, not fruity. John Wayne, our favorite cowboy, strong and typical yet with an apparent romantic side. In westerns seen on his bay horse many times, and it was said he could ride some, in a dismissive way. In his early days Clint Eastwood acted in westerns, smoking six shooters should jog your mind, no butts about it. He played several roles as both a seeker and strong protector. He went on to play numerous character types and then successfully directed some films. Over time he became interested in politics and was elected mayor of Carmel by the Sea, California. Humphrey Bogart, forever dressed well, on and off the screen sharp, our strong silent thinker had a little mystery. Sly explorations, kissed by Lauren Bacall, a face and expression you can forever recall. That one eyebrow says it all. An icon, Steve McQueen, so easy on the eyes, portrays a shrewd calculator, a prisoner and racer that drives with haste and accuracy. Let us look at our funny men. The natural humor of Alan Alda, dreading demise if there's no chance to dance. George Burns, Henny Youngman, Mr. Warmth- Don Rickles. Joan Rivers and Rodney Dangerfield, where's my recognition, they were all funny and fast, making one-liners last. Remember, if you lose a sock in the dryer, it comes back as a Tupperware lid that doesn't fit any of your containers. The Bowery Boys, Laurel and Hardy, and more. The Marx Brothers, a favorite group, is more than fun in Duck Soup. From the early 1930s the 4 brothers made anarchic movies. A Night at the Opera and Horse Feathers are also in the coop.

Some prefer a middle name, look at this expression. The Blonde Bombshell. The only war was against lonely hearts, monks and married men. Did she assault vaults? Diamonds are a girl's best friend, that's Marylin Monroe. With sophisticated class and a little sass here's Grace Kelly and Jane Russel. All beautiful figures. No possible peril to finding a mate, alluring assault with drop-dead weapons, beauty and charisma. Visibly astounding in film, costumed to the hilt, without guilt.

Incredible and uniquely crafted, many by Irene, and Helen Rose. A prize in just your size. Her work was held in esteem, each piece having value in honor and admiration. You would never hear "seam one and you've seen them all." Individuals with talent to spare. Actors sing while some dance, most found time to make romance. Partnered with magnetic empathy. Gene Kelly in my dreams… if I could look deep into his eyes, I would see every celebration of life. Too much energy to burn and pure, natural capacity. I may not have talent, but I could match his inclinations to smile and motivation to move. I have a unique natural dancing style, when I'm on the floor with my husband and the music gets in my groove, I let it take me. John says, "when you start that, I don't know where you're going." Neither do I, the music and my body inspire whatever together. It starts in my feet and hips, goes up to my shoulders, out to my hands then sparks my fingertips. You can trace my suggestion, but even your spirit hasn't mist me yet.

IN THE NO

With the original inclination and invitations created, then sent, the combinations will instil effects. The time has come to regard the undertakings. Comments and reactions, then following consequences should have several results. The replies and arrivals need to be regarded and then any following considerations will have different yet defined relations. Their results should give us a look at association to other guests, also more options of response. Once we dare conversation, we'll be gracious for sharing. To have personal feedback, new hopeful connections may benefit and favor. Exchanging knowledge should bring satisfaction, relieving boredom and possible distraction. The desire for education, to be in the know, is well regarded and links to our endeavor. Having begun we may need a cure from however foreign this weekend occurs. Each invitee is welcome here. Let the outcome during encounters be without any guns. Shooting the breeze is considered okay. Those involved, here by request, have cast their own impressions, and now it's done.

Laid out before you is our host's aim, a will to establish a formula of an original type. A gathering of the very old and not so new, to share ideas and passed paths to understand, dead or alive. The meeting has come through the expression of the mind's eye. The belief that through strong energy, think it and it will happen. With people from almost every walk of life have been researched and now encouraged to attend the affair. Although we are naturally intrusive, there is no need to beware. For your own interest, not in any bank, pay attention and allow yourself to enjoy the fantasy. How can you be homesick when you are here, most of the time, aren't you sick of being there? Do you want to go home or get loaded with bones. Cheers! Skeletons surround the grounds. Come with me, in any dimension and let us be fed by Dinner with the Dead.

Invitations calculatedly sent using awareness and new clues. With investigation and intention, I believe I have not overlooked any troupes or collections. I have given my best interests and intellect, with no desire of steering you wrong. I hope all of those invited know they are wanted. Be free to develop personal thoughts, then set them loose, and assemble as they're sure to grow. The not dead but very welcome, some active people interested in the event. A science enthusiast and astronaut, Brad Carpender. Brad likes to explore everything to the fullest. In space during travel there is time to lend. He opens his mind to life. His heart aches for home and his partner, their nights and desire are intoxicating. So much time apart it seems forever. When home they drink their senses dry. Every way, intellectually and physically, they show their love, pulling it from their souls. Be what you are and do all you can. Let it go!

A landscape artist, sketches, adding watercolor elements, as well as cityscapes and landmarks. Stefani Pagliaro has also dipped in some oil portrait work along with antique jewelry. Her gem is her personality, it draws you beautifully in. Her face is classic, unique and current. Often, she is a magnet, for information and space, you feel you must close into her. Her knowledge, olive skin, love for food and wine all make you feel perfectly fine. Murray Silverstone, a recreational sailor, also tourist passage and destination transport. The breeze, gusting so strong, enticing you with his silver blue eyes, and dark skin heritage, commanding an exotic journey. Samantha Yardley, an Egyptologist, whose special concentration is ancient structures, pharaohs and people. She has learned details of the arts of love from ancient time forward. An English literature graduate, Gabrielle Towers, has special interests in European written fundamental works from thirteen hundred to sixteen hundred AD. This compelling wonder is her sustenance. The few, above exceptional authors, bound her with ropes of sentences. Captivation by her interest is your fare, and its provision. An army man, more than attentive in horseracing and creating metal gadgets, is our Quebecois, Robert Gaucher. Quite rugged, his tanned face with strength throbbing in his forearms, could gently hold you. Forever. I am sure our five, alive, will have some varied interest in these guests. Regardless of the differences in their physical make up. During the gathering, meeting new, and historically true characters, may there be ample illumination to see it through.

Personality contains a world, its own universe, noticeably unique. Over years develop and increase when possibilities allow. Given rules and parameters, take in what is needed and only consider these stems as a start. With imagination, ideas develop and can multiply, so keep all options open. Choice is yours, think of a walk-in encyclopedia with space, a personal world where you can search, then create. Implosion of touch, then the brain explodes with observation. On the inside and out, surveillance with a promise and no debt. Favour and portrayal at times are tied with fear, but here lose your suspicions. What is exterior of us present barriers to endure, catch and conquer. Dying endlessly, why? We'll all end up grey forever, hair, bones and all the earthly physical zones. Exert individuality and learn to overcome without negative development. Engage without requirements if you understand responsibility. On earth life has been a gamble from the start. The time you come from the warmth and support of your mother until you pass from one oasis to what's next. Commit to being you. Intermingling can open doors to comprehension, teach yourself with communication and use it. Coax interaction and coach thought, train with explanation. Understanding can be a hurdle, being patient will help the bulb light up thoughts in your head. One summer day, an evening of fun gets two of us together, friends through work. Athan was pure Grecian art. We hadn't seen each other for a year or two, so there was a lot of catching up to do. During the dark of the night, I had brought a toy to use. A beautifully crafted wand, about the size of a ping pong paddle, its sophisticated shape added to the beauty. From a shining oak handle it was supple lambskin leather on one side and black rabbit fur on the other, so soft on both sides. I used the fur gently, surrounding and patting his buttocks. Once he was in rapture, I turned it over and spanked the lowest portions of his buttocks with the lambskin. I wasn't hurting, just teasing. As his sounds came more quickly, I returned to the side of soft fur. I did this several times before he was spent. Rolling over he said from his damp lips, "Did you take a course?"

Let's get the rest on some more guests. A few facts that were a display of this. Here we go, let's get nosey. In sixteen twenty-four AD New York city was founded. Ages before in Olympia, seven hundred seventy-six BC were the first Olympics. There they used a honey cheesecake as an energy replacement after competitions. I have not thought of this from a health or energy perspective but see something new I have found. I know yogurt is an ingredient having calcium, vitamins and helps the auto immune system. Nutrients support, sports with any stretching, extension, or outdoor activities. Greek style benefits digestion is high in protein, a building block for muscle tissue. Other ingredients and advantages include calcium, helping bones and teeth. This food aids weight loss and heart health. It promotes immune systems with B vitamins including B2, B5 and B12, very good for the skin. Honey is an antibacterial agent. A writer, Athenaeus, discovered the oldest recipe in two hundred and thirty AD. Will it become new again?

From Pella, a city in central Macedonia, Greece. Born in July, three hundred fifty-six BC, Alexander, third king of Macedonia for less than thirteen years. Becoming known as Alexander the Great, the most famous student of Aristotle. After succession he invaded Persia, liberating the Greek Cities in Asia Minor. He then defeated Persians in Egypt, Syria, Mesopotamia, also invading North East Africa. While in Egypt he founded Alexandria his best-known city. His conquests extended eastward taking Bactria and the Punjab. He dyed of fever in Babylon. Regarded as a god in his lifetime and became a model for subsequent imperialist conquerors. A brilliant legend. The "Great" is far from unbelievable! His name was popular in people of rein, poetic literature and health. The Alexander technique promotes body awareness by ensuring minimum effort through maintaining posture while carrying out movement.

Let's make headway to March nineteenth, eighteen thirteen, in Scotland. Dr David Livingstone, a Scottish physician missionary and explorer who exercised western attitudes in Africa. In eighteen fifty-five he was the first European to see Victoria Falls, at the border of Modern Zambia and Zimbabwe, naming them after Queen Victoria. He was interested in meeting new peoples, and in the interior of Africa, freeing them from slavery. In eighteen forty-nine he travelled across the Kalahari sighting the upper Zambezi River. He was the second to see this. Please allow artistic licence and let us move from a physician to a musician, Dr Livingstone to Dr Love.

Two centuries after the conquistadors, for the love of Queen Isabelle, despite her temper, slight as it was. When hosting a sizable dinner party, she confided her complaints. "My whining is only a symptom of responsibility. The duty is killing me." The seventeen fifteen Spanish Treasure fleet was formed. Ships sailing under the command of Don Juan Delila travelled across the world, searching for treasure, gifts for his queen. She was every note, the music of his soul. To South America, Mexico, Peru and the Incas. The Philippines Captain Antonia DaEshavets amassed silver, gold coins, jewelry and pieces of eight. All treasure for the queen's dowery. From the Caribbean around the American peninsula and up the eastern seaboard they sailed. During these efforts torrential rains, relentless wind and hurricanes persistently pounded their ships. The attempted journey home ended there where they were smashed repeatedly on the ridges, banks and reefs. The fallen treasure was plundered and until today people search. Disintegrated metal posts used to hammer the decks together have been found. Some bent and weather worn coins, pieces of gold chain and rare jewelry found are in museums.

Another rhythm, skipping in time, let's move to Stevie Wonder, an American musician, a former child prodigy. Becoming one of the most influential in the twentieth century, with his hits like My Cheri Amour, You are the Sunshine of my Life and Superstition. A superstar, singer and songwriter born six weeks early, lost his sight from high blood pressure in his retinas. All from extra oxygen in the incubator, causing the extreme force. He learned by playing an out of tune piano of a neighbour, then the harmonica, all with his ears and touch. He insisted on completing formal training as a professional. He continued his singing and piano lessons. Even after producing many hits, he took lessons of song writing, if you get a chance tune in. He remarked in an interview at the AOL global greens pre-Oscar party, "After being a vegan for two years, that's helped my already good-looking self." he joked. Eating healthy is a good thing. His music has won the world over since he was popular. If you're looking for royalty, I see the Countess Browse, she has raised them shopping once or twice. The Count patiently waits and will tap his toes now, then more than now. Time flies. Whether you've had fun travelling the seven seas or swinging with the Beach Boys in Hawaii, feel the beating of water, drums and the heart. The sun in a crystal-clear sky quietly waits an escape. A gentle wind starts the sand to fly, over waves of the existential water. The drought and the flood, fearsome from above.

World recalls another conqueror, Genghis Khan. From May third in Temujin, born 1162, he ruled the Mongol empire from 1206, until his death in 1227, he was a man of impressive undertakings. He ruled the land as his empire grew from the Pacific to the Caspian Sea. When not in battle he enjoyed Saki, a Chinese rice wine. Turkendrin, a grape wine was also

drunk in honor of these times. He was known for loud drunk-
enness during common gatherings, singing and dancing.
With magnetic sympathy go back a century to imagine yourself with champagne, flowing with liquid imagination.

SHALL WE GET DOWN TO THE BONES?

If there is a failure to meet and distinguish, trip back and chill
out in the Spirits in Saloon. Who knows which character may
come your way? For seasons and many reasons perhaps perceiv-
ing takes more than time. Let it all go and open seamlessly.
Take place at any table and let's go for a ride. An adjoining
Casino with card tables and a stand-up long oval one for craps,
another, round for roulette. A small low-key band creates
mood, adding to the ambiance. Chips of numerous amounts,
from five dollars to five hundred dollars, are available at the bar,
so good luck to you, but it generally goes to the house. Asking
the past poker king, Henry Orenstein, what brought him here.
His reply was, "the real deal." I took some time in creating and
then assessing specific history and people. A particular arrangement does not allow the freedom people require to circulate;
chance allows an abstract array of encounters. I did not think
it, I know it. When and where you least expect, along it comes.
The welcome here includes the ability to join those of choice,
casually moving through the event. While the banquet is being
served you will be seated with people like yourself that have
made history. Purposely if curiosity kills. Let's await the dinner
party with the dead at the Carnivore Café.

The bells ring and the band starts some jazz, now it's time to dine and partake. Our occasion this evening will help us get to know more people and experience episodes that enlivened other lives. As we grow and experience different aspects, knowledge boosts realization. Fabrication or fact, teacher's pet can pay attention to the cat. Life is a kaleidoscope of colors and force, Leonardo Davinci famously illustrates. The here and now shows love and breath can give. How and why but never when, though one might try again. During the evening eats and facts, you can take note. It is the Who's Who, after they dress, they are fashionably late. Givenchy, Simon Chang, Hugo Boss and Nada, all staged by Debbie Coruzzi, dress to the Nines. Dinner is at eight, while the fragrance of heavenly flavors invite, gesturing you to join. Enjoy what you can and if you're not behind bars, be in one! One can be crazy like a fox, or an outrageous mademoiselle. It doesn't mean you've been to university. Prohibition Edition, not the New York Times, but it was kind of a crime. Was that a bed check or a bad cheque? A circus act, the Bearded Lady, is that above the waist or below. Get a shoeshine for a dime, who has a bootleg to stand on? Cash on the line, an astute prostitute is perhaps your good time. The nineteen twenties flapper girls doing the Charleston, the stockings hold their bankroll. Stocks go down faster than the girls on the street. Due to long speculation in nineteen twenty-nine, the market crashes causing prohibition. The Great Gatsby, a fictional character in a novel by F Scott Fitzgerald written in nineteen twenty-five. A millionaire moonshiner throwing extravagant parties was James

Gatz. Born on a farm in North Dakota to shiftless parents. Ambitious and proud, he went to Lucerne College of Saint Olaf, for only two weeks. Loathing his janitorial work, he became too embarrassed by poverty. Then Dan Cody arrives, a wealthy copper mogul. His amazing yacht dropped anchor, its splendor symbolized wealth. Jay swam out to him to warn of a coming storm, and they become friends. Then Gatsby's girl Daisy later became his undoing. She killed Cody's woman, Myrtle Wilson, driving his 1931 yellow Phantom Sedona Rolls Royce. He was with her, but in trying to protect her, things hit another barrier. Deeply depressed, and one day not well dressed, she was Gatsby's final undoing. Here don't ask Degas to draw. Cody finds an unhappy Jay floating quietly on an air mattress, in the pool where he shoots him, and then himself. I call that a back-handed stroke. This grave story of four had money, love and crime, told with genuine features of the time. What a way to take the air out of your balloon.

MAKE AN ENTRANCE

4pm, in costume or come as you are. Lakshmibai has never been a sorry sight, full of light, in her diaphanous silk sari. The guests have arrived, some their usual sullen self and some smiling. First class movement by the Count Expense train, classic cars, and others elegantly by air. Those coming on their trips were as long as it takes to blink. Here today, gone tomorrow. Remember to think. Ghost cars need no detectors, or police, so come as fast as you like! Both pass and cross the line. We begin to see them one at a time or in pairs, eyes lay on what we couldn't have imagined, their real deal. Without fright or shame, have just make-up, maybe a mustache, hat, curls, sword, guns or gowns, and a few have both, what a sight! Recognized gems in jeweled chests while others carry a token piece of customized clothing, or distinguishing object, identification served. The body is just a very dark outline of the figure, so well characterized, a classy collection of artist's charcoals. Examples are Groucho Marx has glasses and a cigar, Popeye holds his can of spinach. Dean Martin has a Martini glass, of course Louis Armstrong, Satchmo, holds his trumpet. In the deepest shields of night, feel this sight. Their figures have no heat nor real physical meat. Another surprise relating to their life are either still pictures or a running record, like a video inside. Shadows and shades in the everglades. This is not only an image for us, but also a new dimension, for all to see. Some people don't change much, but life goes quickly so the image can move fast depicting occupation and occasions. The desired ability to recognize requires our constant refocusing. It can be hazy and hard to figure out at first, then with blurred understanding clarity clicks in. Like the celebrated remake of a classic movie. Even in the same universe, nothing constant except change. Can we familiarize this extreme stylized fashion? Now we're mingling with the dead. The men merge with us in their mid-twentieth century evening clothes. White dinner jacket, white shirt, black bow tie and black slacks. Next to silk sarongs worn by Egyptians and South Asians from ancient times. A collage, blue blooded aristocrats, the Rat Pack, scientists, medicine and technology.

The ladies leisurely walk in a praise to the rainbow. From a clear, glistening white to a smokey midnight black, including every colour and shade in between. As the sun starts its slow descent into the horizon, soon the sunset will paint the sky with watercolors. Let the games begin. Without any further ado let us let us advance to get watered and fed. Smile, your hostess is a steaming chick. Dinner at ate. Thank you to the memorable men, not so gentle in the bar.

Cocktails at the Spirits in Saloon will help loosen the atmosphere up, now sip, you'll be not so stiff! Our oasis for you. The ghosts, our guests, can shake hands, pat someone on the back, and cheer. Take a blast from the glass or tip champagne to the lips and reminisce. Multiple meetings, still walking and talking. It seems no matter the state of your slate, leave inhibitions aside, stand with them as they are true. Here is a selection for those dropping by, coming from distances, some use the sky. The various glassware, clean and cloudless are prepared for liquid combinations. Not just the glasses but also the guests. We may not know it all yet, but we will feel as we see it. Marc Antony, eager for the evening, walks closely to the Lady of Luxor. He approaches with his bronzed skin and active hair. He looks longingly under his thick lashes at her creamy skin. He reaches to touch her chin and her not so innocent eyes target him. With a slim moist smile she said, careful not to get separated from your heads. As he looked one eyebrow raised, no word came. Continuing, Antony, life is an extreme puzzle, in the big picture, I'd like to get a word in edgewise and say my piece. Menus suggesting post prohibition selections, the most widely held. Shall we start with the more popular cocktail, martini. In 1911, at the Knickerbocker Hotel in New York, a bartender of the same name invented the modern version. This is the dean of aperitif. Taste, effect and size are measured by currant changes in the recipe and admired experience. The original version is costumed with an olive... simply speared is the traditional bond.

CHAPTER 3

A HORSE OF A DIFFERENT COLOUR

Late afternoon In the gardens outside the Inn there are smells from the roses, hydrangea and sense filling gardenias. There are walkways across the largest square in an X formation, coming to a circular wood deck in the center, a pergola curtained with spiderwebs and trellis passageways. Eerie suggestions of shadows surround. Benches within and out of the square give places to lounge and converse. This is the first area outside the back and coming from their rooms are the newest visitors, live, with anticipation. The six of them are out to stretch their legs after their trips, and the unpacking for an unfamiliar weekend. They have freshened up and dressed stylishly simple. A wonderous green garden and lawn spread before them as they leave the sliding glass panels across the ground level of the Inn. This back area is a good place for the group to stroll and ponder the setting they've found themselves in. A light grey gazebo was beckoning. Feeling pleasantly renewed they felt they were ready. Stefani has recently been to Italy to do some studying while visiting family. This was an objective she had for years. To reacquaint, see again and gain the familiarity to do some initial sketches. Each personality bathed the bearer in atmosphere. This would influence the expression, and paint she selected, one influencing the other. The act of art had some proportions, a modified science. Her far look attracted several people passing by. One couple sauntering with imagination spoke, blushing with ingenuity. After a relaxed conversation they invited Stefani to come up and see them sometime. They had an upper apartment with a view matching some of the local artisan pictures. Stephani replied yes and would manage an evening to visit. Something mystic, even magical she could feel coming. Samantha has travelled Egypt researching in her work. The more explorative and professional travelers are Brad, an astronaut, and Murray, the sailor. Not one of these historians, explorers, or journalists had ever heard of such a trip as this. To see and meet people that made history was unbelievable. Both Gabrielle and Robert have been around but not to those extents. This weekend will be different. The invitations and descriptions for this encounter had a defined address yet vague explanation of its probabilities. After walking the perimeter of the square, they went to the center gazebo for a leisurely seat. They explained who they were, and why they had come. As for what they expected, most had no enlightenment, but a few had abstract ideas. The words dead and ghost seemed something out of a book as opposed to reality. Regardless there was a mixture of unsure faces while others seemed quite anxious. The guest list and partially familiar histories had great attraction. While if there was interaction there could be new information and more personal traits. The true behavior of those qualities known previously by historical literature. As intelligent adults they agreed to keep an eye out for each other. Being in touch with the unknown, if there was such possibility, was this weekend's purpose. Each had a written itinerary and seemed game as four bells sounded. Hearing a deeper breath from each other onward they went. I can only hope Shakespeare will pierce me again, with his wonderful words, and pen.

Salutations to you, with appreciation, for joining us at the "Spirits' Saloon" here at the Inn. We understand you had to walk on water to get here, no waxing surfboards, no side-strokes. Our much younger guests, still alive, have made their way into the bar off the square. Arriving at a special portion of the great hall on the top of the opening there is a stone peak on which is written Enter at Your Own Risk. Speaking of chance I always am reminded of my name. Liza Gay de Saliva, as I've said Mom always called me Gay. From the day I was born I have lived with others' questions. I was born in 1960 and long before my name had a meaning of a freedom of happiness and joy. I try hard to live up to it. In the 70's breathe deeply and understand you can never have too much fun. In the 80's you are not only given but also have a choice of attraction. While carrying decades of definitions you learn to take it, with a smile.

A wide-open room where the actual bar area is the back wall. From the left corner going right, wooden shelves holding the red wine selection slide into X shaped cases on their sides. In a similar fashion the liquor bottles are held. At the front of each section a bottle is displayed with some open for use at waist level. On the other half of the back wall, from the center going right, is a clear shelving with glassware. From liqueur, port, wine, brandy and beer steins they are stocked going from the waist up. From the waist down are shelves for any side-ware, mix for drinks and napkins in the center area. On either end are wine, prosecco, champagne and beer preferred cold. Draft kegs are also found here with the serving spigots above. An organized selection of each for serving ease, laid out by the bartenders themselves. There is a long bar of waist height in front of this back wall as a serving area. There is no Prohibition Edition, the New York Times 1920-1933, but it was a kind of crime. The stocks go down faster than the girls on the street. In the United States, everywhere. Canada was so close they must have had some good relations. And someone was making some money, honey.

Guests do sip and stay with their drinks for a time, then move on to a table or meander and meet. The greatest of greetings is recognition, flattering and a compliment. Ignoring someone could be an adventure, perhaps disastrous in nature. If there is none, the evening could be a brisque risk. What the hell. The vision of an attained gathering of varied people was an overwhelming escape. New in nature with no time to waste. Each procured their favorite beverage and had a quick gulp in mind, a shot of becoming ready for anything. Stefani found some of the great painters while Samantha looked for Cleopatra. Brad was trying to find Einstein's trail and Murray looked for the past seaworthy captains. Passed is another reference here. Robert was in search of Caesar or a mounted Antony while Gabrielle was keeping her eyes and ears open for Geoffrey Chaucer. After dismounting, Marc Antony happened along, with his beer Robert spotted him. He walked over and started a conversation, horse oriented. This was a common experience, so they were enjoying their conversation. After a while the discussion moved to women and Antony introduced his love of Cleopatra. This ancient romance Robert had read about and been captivated by it. He was almost making a toast to it while he drank his Hairy Mary. This is a spicy Bloody Mary garnished with a few pieces of plucked hair from the pubic area, ouch! That's a love bite or two. Marc's love then was so strong, and they met many times. Cleopatra why be chaste, when you've been so desired, don't waste. He recalled remarking to her, "May your laughter break through the clouds bringing sunshine". After their relationship had been discovered by Caesar, Cleopatra had an idea of what would befall Antony's behavior. Through their love, beyond strong, he uttered with liquid blue eyes, "May your devotion blanket us no matter the weather." Rather than have her lover go through an agonizing torture, she decided to poison him then have herself bitten by a deadly snake. As he was dying in her arms he said, "We are so close, you and I will make this death nothing more than one life." Such profound care, a relationship astonishing in contrast to others.

They strolled from the bar area through an archway together. True soulmates.

Samantha ponders her work after a hard day, both psychologically and scientifically. She found Cleopatra applying traditional ancient Egyptian makeup. There was a decanter of red wine, so they joined each other in a glass. As the two women acknowledged each other's interests they began a conversation regarding face coloring. Cleopatra used mostly linear black markings with a strong blue shading following the lines. There were hints of red helping to define and accent the facial shaping. Cleopatra said the markings were not for vanity, but respect for the Pharaohs, prior sovereigns and their gods. She asked if Samantha would like to have some applied. This was a great experience for her. It would also be in line with her research, and an honor. Cleopatra started applying markings, slightly different and not as bold in color. She explained the differences were due to the dissimilar age in history and birth line. The god followings had become varied for many of the peoples, over the multiple years, and this was also regarded. Once finished the two beautiful women started sauntering while they were discussing ancient times. They came upon some of the great artists of medieval times. During their introductions Van Gogh remarked on his observation of their face colorations. He was interested in the material used for such decoration. As Cleopatra described natural materials discovered, then combined and pounded to make the different shades. Samantha had questions about his artistic interpretations, also the concern of his depression. Cleopatra dressed for duty with ease, comfort and the touches of splendor came effortlessly. She asked Samantha if she would like a new style of sheath dress. Describing it as a sleek, smooth fabric that would cling in soft places. This is a fitting depiction. Sounding like both comfort and beauty, Samantha smiled. Cleopatra slyly sent her man servant over with a gilded box. Seeming a large container, after asking, Samantha was told it also had dangling jewels for her neck. Pleased and curious she opened the box. The silken fabric, many tints of hazel with gold gossamers, luscious in her hands. She could not resist touching her face with the smooth fabric from threads of purist silk. As she was thanked, Cleopatra curves her defined fig-colored lips, encouraging her friend to try the jewelry. The large glossy stones with velvet colors were a persuasive adornment. She donned them without realizing what the chains were made of. Snakes. They rest with the gems secured. Lovely on her curved collar bones. The living beauties! This was the first jewelry that could poison a woman. Eyes and bodies completely enchanted, a short stinging relationship.

From ancient, beer, wine and grog to the modern Manhattans, Old Fashioneds, Martinis, and Rusty Nails, drinks are enjoyed on many occasions and at several different hours. Five Hundred AD a favorite one to make was fermented spit. Is that an afternoon, mealtime or morning short drink? Frankly I'd rather be lined up than to drink that shot. Morning thirst quenchers can be a Bloody Mary which start simply with tomato juice, harmless enough, to which vodka is added on ice, Worcestershire, horse radish for special spice, cracked pepper on top with a lemon wedge for squeezing. This will, more than often, bury a hangover. Mary the First was the queen of England 1553-1558. She was nicknamed Bloody Mary, for her persecution of protestants, who were burned at the stake by the hundreds. Crispy kabobs by the hearth, warm and content by the yard. Getting back to the drink, the mixed ingredients are a dash of vitamins and wake up call, what a cure. No positive information the drink was named after her. Champagne with fruit juice is not unusual and good use if any leftovers exist. Traditionally since the 1800s champagne with orange juice is a Mimosa. Add a splash of Grand Marnier, that's the key. I prefer champagne and pure pomegranate juice. Pucker up, butter cup!

Some people you think have a good, working brain, but being forgetful creeps up. As time passes, most of us get our share of this trait. Some interesting behaviors show signs of this. As our cocktail party gets into swing, guests move around to meet new people, taking advantage of the gatherings. As they connect and start to chat, they reach for their libation and find it missing. Where did I leave it last, an ongoing question for many. Of all people Benjamin Franklin had so much on his mind, the vessels, in comparison, held little importance. Another unlikely forgetful individual is Shakespeare, with so many words in so many orders, I don't doubt his brains were bogged. So if you were to glance either of them taking a sip, and then responding unusually, there's a chance your drink has been found. Not uncommon in the lounge. There are more absent-minded guests, I am trying to observe, and will let you in soon as possible. Apparently, some traits of the mind continue, they were part of you at the end. Whether alive or dead no addition or subtraction makes you perfect. No names mentioned. Good spirits to you, cheers. Improvement can only help, before the next glass vanishes, poof!

The origin of the term cocktail is a horse with a docked tail, the connection is unknown. I still misunderstand why Adam and Eve did not enjoy apple juice. Yet during their early time, thirst and thought could unearth first formations. Cider anyone? This could encourage inebriation, the initial flight is libation, no lost luggage. Be sure to recover each other. But we will welcome Captain Bligh with a glass of West Indian rum. Once upon a rhyme, it was time to unwind. Murray approaches with a smile and another tankard of rum. Knowing the preference, remembering the choice of seaworthy men. They started a conversation of ship fitting, then views of gaining and training crew. A beaker of wine for Shakespeare, his preference to ale. Along saunters Gabrielle with her favorite wine, always a Spanish red from the Rioja region. Beer was popular in Ancient Egypt for most. While Tutankhamun was known for slaves educated through relations and developed a love of red wine. In these times there were few wells, and it was observed people fell ill after drinking water from the Nile. In this lounge water is overrated, the more you enjoy, the more your true spirit will evolve. I could say awry, but you're already here. Cheers!

Though it can keep you alive, anything aside from red wine for the poet Geoffrey Chaucer. He was awarded a gallon of wine a day, from King Edward the third, as appreciation for his literary creations and help. This was awarded for the rest of Chaucer's life so I'm sure, soon after, he'd rather be dead than drink red. He felt like he was drowning in it but did not go down 3 times. Long after Chaucer who lived in the second half of the 1300s, Armagnac was first developed. Either by boiling down or distilling wine it became a golden brandy made in the 1500s. The original name has come from the Dutch word meaning burnt wine. Going forward into the 1900s the term cognac became used in France. Armagnac was refined in the Gascony region of France in the township of Cognac. The procedure had several steps, requiring specific equipment and time, so was more costly and refined. People of status and perhaps power favored this post dinner specialty in a snifter. Over the years letters appeared on the label after the name. VS, very special, aged at least five years, VSOP very superior old pale, aged twenty years and XO extra old, twenty-five years. Now let's watch out for the bees and have a Stinger. 1 ¾ oz Cognac and 2/3 oz white crème de menthe. Pour over ice in a shaker, vibrate it hard, and strain into a martini glass. If you like you can have it in a rock glass with the ice. In any glass, it's a blast. A votre sante.

Eve was walking fawn-like with eyes wide, this was her first and curious, night away. The language she heard was far from the usual utters from Adam and the sounds of the creatures. She had watched how the other people had lifted glasses, holding while communicating. Then lifting it to the mouth to take sips down. She had been given, the unknown apple, cider in a goblet. Now admired a man with a triangular vessel. The craft and contents were clear, and the man was laughing now and then, a spark in his eyes and a nice smile. She approached him. Dean Martin never loses a beat. He introduced himself as he took in her innocent beauty. Dark auburn plain, long, but silky hair, and her mysterious cedar eyes. Her costume was foliage. She was slow to communicate, her voice wavered. Dean offered his glass and in giving, asked her who she was. Silently, after her first sip, she made a sour face and had an unfamiliar feel in her upper chest, breathing in. Now afraid she looked for somewhere safe and quiet. She did want him to follow unexpectedly so she took his hand. They slipped away trying to show each other their form of exchange. A wide range.

Good thing we have a selection of beverages both worldly and old fashioned. But you'll find no sour whiskey here. If the country starts with a consonant, leave out the e spelling whisky. If the country starts with a vowel, add the e for whiskey. India is the only exception to this rule. Regarding fashion, Crown Royal is a good one, consider the vintage taste. How about a true Margarita? Use 2 parts Don Julio Reposado Tequila, 3-parts fresh lime juice, ½ agave nectar, salt. Tequila poured in a metal shaker, add fresh squeezed lime and agave, then ice. Shake vigorously until chilled and, from the warmth of your hand, diluted. Take a short glass and run a thick lime wedge around the glass, then rim with crushed salt. Pour with metal strainer into the glass with ice, now garnish with a lime wheel. You may be thirsty now, but the work will pay off. You don't need to get to the bank to trust me. Ole. Let's try to Rob Roy. Start with 2 parts single malt whiskey, ¾ part sweet vermouth, 3 dashes of aromatic bitters into a metal glass. Stir until with ice until chilled and diluted. Strain into a cocktail glass, garnish with a maraschino cherry. It's time to try something newer, a Pineapple Daiquiri. With 2 parts medium dark rum, fresh pineapple chunks, ¾ part fresh lemon juice and ¾ part simple syrup. Now pour rum into shaker tin and add 3 pieces fresh pineapple. Add the lemon juice and simple syrup. Fill with ice and agitate until chilled and diluted. Double strain into a cocktail glass. Sweeter for those that prefer it. An Italian Bake. 2 ½ parts Grand Marnier, one part brandy, ½ cup pomegranates, one cup pure pomegranate juice. You can mix in a wine decanter and add enough ice to make more of a "punch"—no gloves. For more than two, multiply the recipe to suit. No martini but still a smart cocktail.

Or using this liquid, pour straight up after chilling. Getting slightly off topic, but this is a dinner, use as a marinade- the other kind of bake- mix the same ingredients and add ½ cup of bone broth, stir and leave at room temp. Preheat oven to three hundred and seventy-five while browning two chicken halves with salt on both sides. Put the cut sides down in an oven pan and spoon some liquid marinade over the halves. Then roast with the rest of the mixture poured in the pan around chicken. Once the chicken is in the oven turn it down to three hundred and twenty-five. Check chicken with a deep cut on leg side after twenty-five minutes, if pink it may need another ten to fifteen minutes. Check after ten because once each leg has been cut and pushed gently to look for pinkish flesh with a deep slit, the heat gets in faster, do not overcook. Deeply delicious. Let's get back to the heart of the matter. Here at the Inn's lounge there's no ordering or expecting a tiny martini. Good luck, and who wants something that doesn't do the job. Go big and stand your ground. Ours is large and true to recipe, packing an afternoon or evening pizazz. No fruit juices, with sweet liqueurs, that's for kids. Grow and suck it up, now enjoy the classic stuff. Getting wet will help you glow, and warm you to the bone. I am not as fresh as I used to be and will start with a dry sparkling white or pro-secco. If eating Greek, I'll turn my chin to the ceiling, then have Ouzo poured into my mouth with a pillow behind my head. Swallow before it overflows. This direct and fulfilling act should soon be accompanied by dishes of Mediterranean fare. Eat slowly as you savor the flavors of all regions. The music rises then a plate smashes on a white firepit! If choos-ing Italian, please start with two parts Grappa shaken with enough ice to dilute, then strain. If this doesn't wake you, Frankenstein's parts and sparks won't either. Brad Carpender where for art thou and thy chemistry set. Quelle dommage. The nickname for the bar is the Formaldehyde General. This hospital specializes in plastic surgery, you will look and be well preserved.

Ben Franklin took such a great pleasure from wine he penned a song in praise of drinking it over drinking water. My kind of guy! His wine collection and knowledge helped him in his role as American Minister to France. It didn't hurt in aid of the French taking him seriously. Einstein had a coffee and tea preference, known to have once drank them simultaneously. No stein for Einstein... caffeine freak? Tastebuds desolate but thoughts promising. Results indicate potential. Those ingredients can be the base for the famous Spanish Coffee, coffee with Kahlua, Triple Sec and rum. Thanks to Captain Edward Teach, known as Blackbeard, that demon rum shows up time and time again! You don't have to hold back but don't leave your hands on his flask too long... Keeping with caffeine are the makings of a Blueberry Tea. One cup of Earl Grey tea, add ½ oz Amaretto and ½ oz of Grand Marnier. Either on a cold day or a hot night it keeps the cobwebs away, and you awake. Back to where the not so gentle men were from, generally ale drinkers. They're also known to have a glass of wine or a cognac, but only sipped what was served. To abandon fogginess, I do suggest putting that blueberry tea to the test, on your palate and headache. Amuse your mind, mouth and self. There's another chapter... Appropriate to wine and later dine.

Vincent van Gogh and Picasso both were interested in Absinthe, a fascinating history. Considered to be dangerous, as a highly addictive drug with psychoactive and hallucinogenic properties. A green, aromatic liqueur, 68 % alcohol made with wormwood and other herbs, having a bitter licorice taste. Now banned in western countries, if you can lay your hands on this do not be coward of these qualities. Using this once in a while as it wasn't lethal, ingredients and process of distilling and bottling, in 200 or more years can change things. Back when these artists were living the dream, doing it a few times, you could experience those properties if art, design or imagination is part of your life. The right brain dominating the left brain. In everyday practice Picasso pleased himself with Catalan sausage and beans. But mostly living on fresh fish, a little wine, fruit and vegetables. Although a simple nutritional regime he lived 91 years even using the liquor now and then, maybe with a pencil or brush in his hand. Until 1973 food was the constant touch stone in art and his life. Let us step aside for a moment. Of all the people you've met, all the conversations have brought an entrance. Whether educated or not, you used your interest to open and have passed through. Life can suddenly change, so use a moment of to get there. Make the most of days you have so go ahead, tint and decorate with your personality. Let your son shine.

A Calgarian rodeo femme fatal could bring Julius, the Caesar, a most popular cocktail of our time. Calamity gained! Walter Chell, the inventor, rimmed a glass with celery salt, then adding ice, vodka and clamato juice, a shot or two of Worcestershire. My augmentation is horse radish, a sharp spicey prick helps infuse flavor. Stab a sprig of blanched asparagus and attach it to a celery spear. Use this to stir, then munch on. This situation brings the emperor readily able for action, an endeavor of taste and bravery. These men of true character bantered back and forth about past atmospheres alongside their courage. With beverages warming old strains, calmness brought much description to each scheme. The typical use of hands when conversing aided wine and ale to slosh in goblets, and, of course, themselves. All while standing tall enough for the others to look up to. The droplets and stains showed sign of boisterous, bragging rights. A cordial and fortunate sight, what spirit! As our guests continue mingling in this affair it is an interesting fact to see the drink and food travel down the throat. It reaches a storing spot and I have yet to see how it is digested. A vanishing act? One hopes. They smile, talk, stroll and are as amazed at how this function has succeeded. Exceptional. Weave threads from thoughts for a living fabric. Intention becomes inspiration. The only invisible figures are those who chose not to come. I would not be surprised in a sixth dimension, from what I have learned and seen. Its existence, concepts to inspire, then accept. Over countless centuries there still may be a dedication to vocation. Any axes to grind should have wound down. Embarrassed by the running film of life in them could be an excuse. Feeling an invitation to share a dangerous secret, or even a selfless duty. No need to be a coward. Think of time eating you alive, isn't there somebody better?

Those new to their death had some interest in the other ghosts. The conversations shot on, diverse groups, good dissimilar anecdotes. A group of men met once a month to enjoy, among other things, sour mash whiskey in short and sturdy rock glasses. One evening Giuseppe Joe Aiello arrived in a mid-colored suit, top hat, grey gloves and a walking stick, a respectable look for the occasion. These men met at the Cleveland Hilton in the lobby bar. Irving Feinstein went up the carpeted stairs, decorated with largely spaced circular shapes. A host held his hands out for the hat, gloves and walking stick. Given a claim check, he had no reason to ask where he was going, this group was well known. Aiello joined the men at a spherical table and sat in the last empty seat. The distinctive conversation was shared and noted on all sides, it was a continuation of the previous month. The words were swallowed along with the martinis, beer or whiskey in front of them. At the point when there was no more to add that evening and a good start for the next, they finished their night. As the men left for the door there was a separate exchange going on. The host handed him his outerwear as they started down the few stairs of the foyer. At the base of the steps the conversation lulled after most of the group gave a single nod. Giuseppe Joe discretely pulled a small pistol from his jacket and shot the man opposite in the upper arm. After the small blast no one looked surprised, including the staff, and the blood spilled from the man's jacket beginning to pool on the carpet. His arm was held tight with a handkerchief from his pocket, and he was helped out of the hotel. The men left by groups into waiting cars. One an antique, the driver up front where roofless, while the cab was covered and sat 4 men. Anticipation of numerous vehicles leading police cars, a waiting taxi was also incorporated. They were driven away roughly at the same time. In the hotel a maid put several tablecloths on the rug to soak the blood, then used a soapy cloth to dab it up, best as possible. Regardless of the effort a large, faded ring shape was left to dry onto the carpet. The entrance to the Hilton with the original simple pattern, and what was left of the blood's faint outer edges became known as the rose. Life went on in the same manner with some similar meetings and beverages. During and after prohibition, in the bootlegging and firearm business Aiello did rise. He also had sights set on higher positions in this growing community of Cleveland. His profession and this story were always referred to as the bouquet in arms. But we're here for beer! Remember it with a short glass of sour mash whiskey while retelling with a lowkey voice. Cheers.

Ella Jane Fitzgerald, born April twenty fifth, 1917. An American Jazz singer sometimes referred to as Lady Ella, the first lady of song and the Queen of Jazz. Known for having pure tone, impeccable diction, phrasing, timing and improvisation especially in scat singing. Wetting her whistle was necessary so often there was always liquid within hand's reach. Her achievements were two hundred albums, two thousand songs, her last recording in nineteen eighty-nine and last performance in nineteen ninety-one. Passing away in nineteen ninety-six, some of her famous songs were Cheek to Cheek, A Tisket a Tasket and You Can't Take That Away. Her legendary pairing with Louis Armstrong from 1946 recording The Nearest of You, Have Yourself a Merry Little Christmas and Autumn in New York, lifts you up when you are down. More of their famous poetry, Lovers in the dark on the bench in the park. Lovers without a dream, need no castle in Spain. Born August fourth 1901 in New Orleans, Louis celebrated red beans and rice, asking his wife Lucille to prepare them before he would propose! He loved to eat almost as much as he loved to play. Famed for Hello Dolly, What a Wonderful

World, That Lucky Old Sun, such beautiful words and a melody that makes you say how do you do. It really means I love you, oh yeah. If we have all the time in the world and all the love, we need nothing more, and nothing less. Music primarily recorded by RCA, Sony, Warner, CBS, Virgin, Vita Phone, MCO and Columbia were the biggest producers of this age. Smaller and some newer are RCO, EMI and TKO. Music in the background, let's get to the beverages, Pass the Sazerac, a local variation of a cognac or whiskey cocktail from New Orleans. Named for the original brand Paul Sazerac de Forget. Have a sip and you'll start smiling under your Mardi Gras umbrella. It's not just the sun that heats you up in New Orleans as the first line passes. Keep rhythm while moving along. It's quite a day! Each year always brings more new music and compilations. Creativity, joyfulness and love bring inspiration. Hear the words and feel the beat, shuffling along the first line on the street. Revel and take pleasure in the musical revolutions, from vinyl albums to CDs, to audio cassettes. Lots of live horns, drums and vocals here! It's all there for the picking.

Latuna, Mexico where El Chapo was born as Joaquin Guzman Laura. He started in a cartel dealing illegal substances. He became a drug lord with mass cocaine, marijuana and meth amphetamine. So much was smuggled, he turned it into a global marketing cartel, once in the US, from the United States to Europe. $$$ Danger, dead man's curve. Enemies evolve, trained rivals an endless adversary. Lifelong competition between them, not for fame, all for retirement benefits. Sometimes early. Notorious fortune, what a tough way to make a living. Time to talk about tequila. His daughter launched this liquor under the brand name Tequila D' El Chapo. Salt on the crook between the thumb and the forefinger, fresh lime wedge and El Patron Tequila. Lick, suck and shoot! Scandalous and a wild way to travel out of boredom! Now there's fortune. In the 1900s draw a powdery white straight line, indulge and support him. Now in the late twentieth to the twenty-first century many of us have daily, simple to complex, needs health wise. Taking medications twice a day and with pollution and pollen, possibly add inhalers, and puffers. Count the number of artificial substances used for multiple reasons including inflammation and pain. Vitamins are for most people, yet how they are processed, and the additives can be harmful. Also used frequently are ointments for blisters, insect bites, pimples and boils… skin cancer melanoma and eczema. Then aging skin, there are many different types of moisturizing cream. How about the old school remedies, such as peppermint for stomach and headaches, used from the times of ancient Greeks? Oils, tea or schnapps from Grandma's recipe, and Mom's favorite education/ lotion for good skin, rosewater and glycerin. Aloe vera from the inside of a fresh plant works wonders on cuts, scrapes and burns, also found in skin products. Dr McGillicuddy's total Health liquid in the old west, sold in small dark blue bottles. Ages ago sold from a stagecoach, at the fair or in the circus, was generally made with moonshine and a few herbs. All for only 10 sense a bottle.

Stalin, born in Gori, 1878, spoke Russian, German and Georgian. Although he and Vladimir Lenin shared the initial communist concept, he was not the director until Lenin's death. Sharing ideas, they on occasion would bend an arm. Vodka was the mainstay and was drank straight, on the rocks, and as cold as their dead. How do skunks come up smelling like a rose, with lies and the eventual acceptance, drunk. The writings of Karl Marx. one of the influences, just kept his bottle outside. When concoctions became popular in the 20th century, the Establishment beverage list was vast and varied. The oldest recipes had less sugar, even the Mint Julep. Then the Long Island Iced Tea and Apple Martini. The latter being 3 parts vodka, ½ oz apple schnapps, the same dash of Cointreau and Calvados. Ice is easy to find, shake them together and get blitzed! Another favorite is three parts vodka to ¾ oz Kahlua. A heart felt oomph touched with the dark and sweet, the Blank Russian. Politically correct. You can always run with a Greyhound, vodka and grapefruit juice. A taste-treat before the Atom Bomb. There's a good name for a shooter, let's mix Jägermeister and Gold-Schlager. If you have a moment, ice it before pouring into shot glasses. I'd say in a split second, but the second could get you smashed. I hope you have insurance.

Hiro Hito, 25 years old in nineteen twenty-six became emperor after his father's death. During WWII, he presided over invading China, the bombing of Pearl Harbor and Japan's eventual surrender. Not known as a frequent drinker yet how many sips of Saki sank the ships in that peaceful harbor. Rice wine is best served heated in thick pottery vases with small spouts keeping the liquid warm. Kampai! Short, small-scale cups of the same stoneware receive the steaming wine which dampened sympathy and enliven their belief in triumph. Here in the Spirits lounge any surrender is your choice, enticed by personal decisions. Our reward is the contribution to a savory and amusing experience. An agreeable education has been the aim. Giving respect to history, both to homage and harm, here wars are not now ours.

This relaxation tradition can develop an addiction. After days of work, designing action, flavors and company could be the attraction. The Happy Hour ritual is in the hands, and chalice, of the individual. The custom of a pitcher of beer, wine or martinis between friends can ease tongues. News may apply to tempt viewing fresh mannerism. This is a beneficial event either out at your favorite spot, or in a familiar home. Who will take an educated guess, moisten your lips, hours less sour.

Bring us around or two, no shots fired, Tequila excepted. Let us encourage and enjoy this gathering, let loose with your visible clues. Some of you know ways to artistically steal the stored. Resurrect, in a tall glass, cold enough to have condensation. Good grief let's catch a thief. Come alive with Bonnie and Clyde. Her semi-automatic gun and his Browning rifle. With his barrel, blow off some steam, what a ride. Jesse James with his Colt 45 Peacemaker, its origins dating to eighteen seventy-two. The Pink Panther Harry Winston heist. How about a revolutionary round? George Washington, Abigail Adams, Benjamin Franklin, Thomas Jefferson and others.

Would use courage, patriotism and gained prominence creating a country and saving its land. Beer, cider or whiskey acceptable. Let the moonshine at night.

Whether or not you imbibe you will enjoy The Hurricane. Two kinds of rum, lime juice, orange juice, passion fruit puree and simple syrup. Will it rock your brain? Sipping a good Mint Julep can resuscitate. It may be a killer but remember the old Italian will, after the game the king and pawn go into to the same box. Gone With the Wind, in a shimmering pint of draught. The cooler king from the movie The Great Escape, Steve McQueen, let off steam often with a stein. A cold beer, now Old Milwaukee cans, his favorite. Then in the 60s he was unrestricted, principally ready to launch. Any way to get off the ground after putting himself 8 ounces deep with his regular medication. As a young man motorcycles and airplanes his interests, what a mover. Then as a marine he liked to get his ship together and get away from the dock. The kitchen is almost ready so after drinks let's eat, time to steady. Wine's always fine with food, they set the mood. Electrify the neurons, a clever cure to everything endured. It may have been your initial visit to the Saloon, the ambiance was what I could give you. Interest and information. Tarzan comes with Jane, how often? For many it is a timeless question, is there a desired answer. Here the bar is being tended by gorgeous Stella, who is very familiar to me. Then enter the Mrs. who used to be a Mr, you know how things can change. Back to our ageless beauty who kindly makes a round of beverages, smart three-ounce martinis. Some favor the famous Caesar, not everyone's style, we smile and happily accept her knowledge and keep on talking. She knows how to please so well, she's created a recipe, like herself sly but not silent. Knowing the love of spice, despite any hour or condition, a tweak to the Caesar, for the ones that like them, has been made. The Wasabi Caesar. To the traditional recipe she adds a small, pounded piece of wasabi paste letting the heat and ingredients infuse. Yahoo, the drink is as hot as Stella is. Her deep amber eyes, surrounded by luscious lashes, long jet-black hair and pure ruby lips. The ones on her face. Back to the promising drink, after the celery is placed in, it's topped with a drizzle of Saki and a crush of dried seaweed, introducing more flavor. Stir before the first taste. This may not be your key but will tune you right in.

Doubles: Cleopatra and Antony. Possibly scandalous talk, so will William Tell? Bogart and Bacall. Bogart dressed to perfection every day. Bacall had compliments her entire life. In the Daily Telegraph, printed 2/3 1988, "I think your whole life shows in your face and you should be proud of that,". Signing a will? It's a dead giveaway. You'll need to make your Marx, Brother. May your brain and thirst be quenched by having Wiser's on the rocks, it will knock you, not up. Open those eyes to take it all in. Some might attempt to make this a surprise party. Several, even countless, could have reasons to disguise, even ages past.

Samantha, a realist looked for clues and found specimens a thousand years ago, no surprise they existed, but what excitement! Known as a renowned archeologist, this hard line of work included years of research, and endless physical input.

Literally digging for clues, the sifting of countless pounds of sand. Feeling some things with fingers rubbed hard enough to bleed by her gloves. In trenches shifting an inch at a time in search of more evidence, above and below. The sun limitlessly bouncing off the world of the ancient desert. Like a stove the heat came almost to a boil. The sand shimmering endlessly, always dry and glinting. Shades for the glaring sun of the shifting silt, either by manual movement or the breezes, at times strong. Strands of hair, wet with perspiration, from the temperature and grueling work. Breathlessly she swiped at them to keep looking, her hype. To wrap them into a ponytail she used the string that was cinching the waist of her pants. Too tight and warm now to work in this harsh heat, now a bit of relief. On manmade steps, with small swept pebbles, she held her arms out for balance to maneuver the spaces. Up and down, bending while exhausted to gently search without pausing. A matchless exhilaration in her to unearth, finding physical history in the field. Uncover and discover. Bringing to light classic, unchanging pieces of our lifelong puzzle.

Totally spent, feeling wasted and pushed to the physical limit, there was no place to go. She stripped her dirty clothes, shaking the dust and dirt off them then tossed them in the basket of worn-out laundry. After a quick and almost cold shower, washed and rinsed, she watched the dirt swirl down the drain. She wearily sauntered to her small room and lay on the cooler sheets of her bed. Spread eagle and sighing in relief. Samantha rolled over taking the top sheet with her, feeling like her lithe body and damp hair were in a cocoon. She breathed regularly and fell asleep. Her broken dreams held portions of the hardest exertions of her arms when digging. Often soft skin was ravaged by the effects of the dry sand and air, the ache of muscles carrying an unknown object. It held possibilities of a new manmade level, stair or even a treasure of significant age. Between waking for relief or just to change positions with ease she fell back into the deepest sleep. These dreams intertwined with thoughts of a rest from this work. Arts and literature drifted in and out of her thoughts. Laying on a lounge chair she was so close to the water, she could hear gulls in the distance, almost mesmerizing. Letters, a written line or two, some by hand drifted in and out of her head above the cool drink on her side table. In this languid state, almost falling away from her daily self she felt the presence of a man coming close. She opened her eyes, slits in the sunlight, and barely twisted her head. Hypnotically Shakespeare nodded and sat sideways, facing her, on a lounge chair so he could communicate. This was relieving, inviting and had possibilities, this was no nightmare. And what an appealing dessert.

WEAR IS THE SEX? I'D LOVE TO TRY IT ON

Some place in life you can remember the first feel of a happy spark. Light yet spirited right from the start. It usually brings life to both your outer flesh and the nether regions. The facial skin gets a fresh rose or peach color while eyes brighten with a trigger. The lower region has an under-surface pull. Slight but noticeable, it slinks forward, compelling hard thuds of heartbeat. Sometimes it is a definite magnetic spark, like an electric exclamation mark! This is just the beginning of the melding of the loins. What is a good account without mystery and love? Honestly once I had an orgasm, it accompanied an explosion; so any mystery was history. For some lovers Xample did not always mark the spot.

No matter what caused the initiation, the feeling began. There is no method, mentally or physically, to stop this most basic action. **H**ow does this start, I like to think it's part of the big bang. Now we are in the dead zone, does one use this part of nature? The get go then stop, go again, full stop. Why would you not want to have this desire? How could it ever end. As a younger woman I was captivated by this spontaneous energy. It was an uninitiated and sudden charge, both internally and externally. The first feelings were from my lowest inner tissue, then sexual organs; a hydrogen atom flowing outward. Yet it came so infrequently, I was always surprised, and taken by it. I had no clear idea of how to explore the craving. I felt as if it was fleeting yet strong enough to register through my entire body. Genuine care and ideas shared could be the score. Where is the love, it was in the making. It came, introducing instant impulse, and there my strong senses originated. The urges became frequent and sharply felt. I knew others were aware of that nature coming from me. There was actual voltage in my body and exchanges. Whether in conversation, enjoying food and beverage, and especially dancing. Rhythm and music were in me, passionately. I had much to share, character bared.

I have no wish to end the gift I was given and why would you? When in the post life partition, I have learned the ability to watch one's life, acts and portraits. Those run through at a constant rate, with no defined speed. One day I was altered, not alone and another was strongly affected. At times during the day, and every night, the pain rips me to the bone. So much so, I have trouble talking about it as it sucks me dry. Certain charismatic moments are apparent, even hypnotic. With the infinite knowledge I have gained in this interlude I find it hard to believe in any imaginable end. A man, woman or small grouping could either tell or show me more. Torture to the core.

Curiosity could kill the cat, but it won't punish the kitten. Cary Grant had captivating eyes, a desirable feature in his chin and is above averagely handsome. By this attraction you could be moved in his optimistic presence and shared good humor. And to my delight here he strolls. Drawn by my thoughts and inquisitive looks at those around the event his appearance arouses my interest. We greet each other with introductions and share some champagne. He can see I am still living so I explain I am the host of this engagement. After having enjoyed his acting career, it is my pleasure to meet him. Many of his works come to mind, good memories. So many movies, comedies, life stories, mysteries, and action. His face is a magical magnet, and manners, charming. He makes you feel like you are the only person in the world. We discuss different occasions in our personal lives from daily duties to professional steam. Few are masked. From one decade and

DINNER WITH THE DEAD

task to the next, probable function to responsibility. Many obligations were by choice and fun; my levy for the use of the word masked.

So, I ask, "Now since things have changed, do you still enjoy another in a natural or sexual way? Is it an intimation, a verbal or physical expression?" His eyes widened to an almost surprised look as his chest rose and fell. "Are you going to take a breath?" he said. Maybe this was the wrong, or too strong an approach. He didn't leave though. I replied, "Yes I will be patient and wait for some verbal information." He seemed sympathetic to my inquiries and compassionately led me to a table with chairs. A true gentleman, he held the seat for me. As he sat to converse, I nodded for him to start. "I have never represented a character in film, or life, a man with raw sexual attraction. I am more a version of charisma and appeal. If I appeared tempting the fascination came from surrounding cast. I have not been without company and physical interaction, so I may be able to give some light, Liza." Being eager to have a leash on this liberation, I politely thank him and ask him to call me Gay. I have no desire to overwhelm him with any female prowess. I casually give him time by glancing around, taking in the evening and the play of guests. I then had a sip of my shining champagne. He briefly gives a light touch to my hand and takes a slow breath. Showing my full attention, I make direct contact with my richly dark brown eyes and smile. "Intimate relations are similar but have a different fashion. Attraction comes naturally as there is no stopping biology and the electrical spontaneity of the body. When people communicate their dealings can deepen. If it consumes time and generates more energy, another level may come. If apparent mutual magnetism is felt it could be communicated by a simple physical movement like closing quarters. The watching and pleasurable regard to the visual past experiences showing in the body is another noticeable step. Then there is potential for an assured contact, a completion of ability."

I nod as I take this in, also imagining these suggestions. I envision this is a road to tantric, the awakening of the female energy. "Do you have a question as I see your mental observations." In my mind my lips are wet but, I have an unusually dry throat and mouth. I don't think I'm at a loss for words, but I take a moment before I speak. There is more to ask and relate. "Is this a mental initiation to secure further engagement? More of a tantric concept and will it be combined, or involve, any physical merging? Does it still have the captivating urgency for accomplishment? Is there, for lack of better words, an internal Roman candle and a guttural scream?" Cut, to the dinner scene…

Hot tropics are not on the dinner menu, but perhaps on another… Not gossip but a good round about talk. Information luring and spicy, not to be purposely nice. Simply a chat, hot, small pieces to know and hear… all about that my dear. Spontaneous temptress, you can see her swallowing it down, so low. For her it's the best, her natural flow. Sparkle with that curved, sly smile, it's a coming party or fest. Get into the music above and below. Think of these things, please be my guest. The highest heavens my only quest.

Yes, on another plane, and that is almost hard to explain. You can see the difference between you and I; the living and the dead, it is on a separate but equal level. Different with similarities. Also, people who have missed each other in life, time, place or people can find one another here. This is where things, thought finished or not possible, can be accomplished. This is a new place and way to realize. Here, as at your home, you can absorb. Try to identify with what you take in, think and figure out.

Two people are two spirits made up of unique charges, and character. They give to each other often if possible, pushing superficial commitments aside to succeed. Achieve beauty, like the strings give to the harp and the tone to the keys on a piano. This is not an out of the ordinary description, being truthful, there is very romantic music to make. It is not a surround and penetrate concept. It is more of an exposure and release, of innermost energy and character, with reserved motion. The intention to draw desire and a connection to the universal drive. A link between the two will gain momentum. The resource can keep giving from deep within. Vitality started so long ago yet the first piece of life is in you. How low can one go? Mysterious but profound are the meaningful layers existing. Instinct so far inside, internal urge to thrust outward every atom. Are you ready to willingly receive and trust the energy will transport the smallest portions of power you are able to open? Having this ability is the guide. Being able to steer the production back and forth is the outer limit. Give and accept, both have the power. The play of the various surges of distinctive qualities, some sparked and others unchanged. Together when reaching their plateau, the diversity dances along with the loud cracks of fireworks. Electrical brilliance both in colors and temperature. As the burning of the gunpowder lights the cool depth of the sky. The explosion!... Affiliation brings a relationship, endlessly filling required targets. In life, also in death, differences can attract like the magnets of the poles, connecting opposite ends of the earth. A serious transaction for the meaning of love, attraction, the closeness of body and soul. They who have been willingly or unnaturally pulled into play, watch each other for a while taking in the person's outline and energy. The moving picture of their life, love, occupation, and friends. Their personal reel without end gives insight to the very essence. When ready to be together, standing, they get close enough to read each other's eyes. Keeping about 8 inches away they move their hands, and this is how they feel each other. Everywhere. They do get their faces close enough to kiss, no press-face, a real kiss. Not everlasting but meaningful, with depth of dedication. The following are words of a special note.

"These Are Our Hours"

Was it History or hers
Some are young, others have been long
Facts of history have featured mysteries
What comes next could be the best
Don't be coy, employ that noise
Come on boys let's hear your voice

Open those doors we will be floored
Make your choice then plot a course
Get on your horse jaunt from the north
Ride hard and fast but make things last
Resources of force from an unknown source
For all times, yours and mine
Take a chance and come along
From underground comes the sound
Activate your hum until it vibrates around
Make this song so good and strong
We are all aware, explode and declare
To this song we can all belong
The past persists to see what is best
No matter the crowd, do not be confound
Search for romance then to love be bound
Strengthen your pace, find it with grace
Show us the dance from here to beyond
Let us feel the joy from each small noise
Heartfelt and meaningful in every voice
From our lips and flesh the tones are fresh
At long last can see to pass those tests
After blessed gifts and miseries confessed
Though some without sass or imagination text
Don't live with glass you could get smashed
Years have brought some glory with this we soar
Forever more you can not measure our roar
You will hear this song for together we are strong

Bridging back to the song

The time is now, the hours are ours
Okay, let's make some noise
Make a choice, give all your voice
The heart of this song is good and strong
Consider the truth, it isn't wrong
Don't strain your brain, just sing this refrain
It's genuine, but seems very plain
Knowledge of extensive travel
Can now be unravelled
What has passed, at long last
Come sail beneath the tallest mast
You'll find we're diamonds
A cast of many thousands
As your hosts we can say you're the most
We can be loud and very proud
We sing these notes while we boast
This tune showers: the song is ours

Making love is the art of every proton, neutron and electron; molecules and rays of light on a merry-go-round, spinning, charging, touching and releasing. Have you seen the shimmering sheen, and can you feel the ice-cold steel? Dead or alive, just before the stars collide. His attention to my probing queries gave real answers and a total view of being out of this world. My desire to experience this extreme and extraordinary intimate encounter blew my mind. I wish he could look right into my eyes and see my dreams. My face shone with the truth and excitement of total understanding. I was thrilled and felt confident in my life, now and the next. Without boundaries I hope to see a sky full of firecrackers this weekend. Knowledge is a good thing. Let the music penetrate, then dance with romance. Make and take it beyond the limit. It's a sensation! Have no fear, come across.

The best conclusion brought a continuation. The day my first husband and I planned, then executed the initial trial to have a baby. I had done research of menstrual cycles to pick days that were optimal. I also read about better ways, days and methods for sperm strength. Now let's leave the clinical side and think of a night with dusk passing and the stars becoming intense. As we came to a marvelous mutual conclusion, another brilliant internal explosion erupted. An enormous feeling and sight in my body and mind participated in a total production of elevation, nothing I could have comprehended. This formed, and surrounding universe was my son's creation. Wow, that was Max's beginning... a new world. As my tummy grew, when resting I would lay on the couch, reading new children's books, gently rubbing my blossoming body. After a few more months of a gently kicking baby, inside a growing mommy, a son was born on April 25, 1992. How could anyone know what kind of energy they were generating?

His creation launched the wonder of a new person who set into motion the biggest joy, tears and many years. Adjustment to new customs, loving care and hours, most sweet and few sour. I breast fed him for a while and as he was drinking my milk, it was lovely and close. It was draining me because I ate like a horse. There were times when nursing I needed to tidy his room upstairs, or the kitchen. So, while he was still small, I could hold him in one arm while he rested, and use the other arm carefully... to fold, clean surfaces, eat or run the vacuum. Multi-tasking with fond mindfulness. Even setting the table for dinner and putting veggies into the sink was after he was burped and put down. I read to him a lot, he smiled and laughed when I used special voices, "come out, come out, wherever you are", and it helped him to rest too. The last line, "I love you up to the moon and back", my favorite book to read him, day or night. Sleep tight. He learned with nurturing attention to do everything with politeness and concern for others. He was smart, learning his letters and numbers completely by his 3rd birthday. He loved books and even had a puffy, plastic one for the bath. It was to get reading familiar and underway. I started buying children's literature as we shopped, and when friends asked what to get as a presents, I easily said books. He had a large selection of many to read before bed. He even asked for a flashlight in case he woke up at night and wanted to read, even under the covers. Honestly, that's Max. Life went on until just after he turned seven, I had a serious accident that changed me and our world together. He and I were both torn, apart mostly. I was unbalanced and then a health side effect changed me. He was moved by his father, to live on an acreage, where he grew up. There is so much left unsaid and truly unknown. Not everything, but the love stems from us. Max's beginning saved my end, that I know. My mother protected my butt many times and I tried my best to rescue hers and give her what she wanted. I am not perfect and have made mistakes. Far away Max grew to get a college degree then afterwards become a journeyman electrician. He has now married a smart and beautiful woman. We may be and live apart, no question. Forever we are a part of each other. Those facts are the truest feelings we know.

CHAPTER 4

THE SLIDING DOOR

As our guests mingle both historic and fresh, they sit and converse or saunter through the grounds. Introductions are followed by chronicles and inquiries. As they relax, refreshed by their favorite liquid, there is time for relating. There is another set of magnets totally unalike. In politics, power, religion and people of dissimilar backgrounds and birthplaces; this can cause a static more than a years' worth of thunder and lightning. Strolling through an archway there is a sudden breath and a deep heartbeat that is both brutal and cruel. A feeling of a total exhale and a new lungful simultaneously. An opalescence surrounds and in an instant existence has been reembraced. As previously described the guests, mostly ghosts, appear as an outline of themselves with a series of portraits or moving representations within. Fathom the rhythm and sight of this different kingdom. When crossing a doorway together this entry replaces the human form, replicating a new ghostly appearance. The persons look like their lives now are duplicated in this manner. Prints run through them as the years had with events, work, family and friends. Interests, education and exploration are relived. From daily occurrences to special occasions, the memories run through, or are rested to show off. What a transformation and spectacle. It takes a few minutes to adjust to the new carriage and hard to take your eyes off the portraits and movie of your life. Whew. Both a new feeling and phase, a fresh gulp of the unknown. Brad Carpender, walking with Albert Einstein, asked with amazement what was happening. Einstein explained the travelling transformation that occurs when escorted by a person, past. Astonishing as it was, the effect is the result of closeness with another energy. This outcome can be if one wishes or does not cross another door. Passing through an entrance with someone of opposing stance is the threshold of change. A revolving door has been accomplished, but the result is quite taxing. Rock and roll. It is much better to experience slowly and one step at a time. Converse and learn life events with one, or many, is an enjoyable experience and show of happenings. It takes effort and time to watch and learn. Life has many splendid episodes. There is a level of ability involved for multiple standpoints. Take a new view of the passing perspectives. Learn the world as it has been for eons or one position and moment. That choice is yours. Preceding histories, persons and places.

Life could be long and full of diverse experiences. If there are good moments, better. Inspire them. Those bright stars will keep you going. You know it so try. My mind is a work in progress, as the years pass. There will always be a scar. I am aware of my body. Everyone has traits to deal with, physical frame and mind. To have inflammation, daily swimming eases pain and exercises limbs. Floatation takes pressure away so the ability to move with confidence allows a solid effort for the best outcome. Sounds like a lifelong renovation. Will physical conditions ever stop? What has happened due to my brain, and life I can't change now, do wishes ever come true? I hope and think positively now. I want to ask about actual death. How does it feel, like a passage somewhere? A dream or a nightmare, does this have to do with the cause. If by disease, will a possible eternity of pain be partnered. If by some physical disorder, is it by an unconscious clearance. Or is it painless, when instantly, if you were killed in war, in the air or on ground. Murdered, in what fashion, knife, gun or by hand and for what, by who. Pain relates to the instrument; it could be fast or slow. Torture, body forces the mind to attend, that I know firsthand. Tell me what conditions go by. How am I overtaken. What elapses in these significant moments? So many critical questions and each person has specific answers. For all of those involved, and the descriptions, a rotating belt for the people and a blade for the answers. Will I see and feel what it is I have missed, will I be forgiven for mistakes, however stupid? Can I learn more?! I believe now I can see others, dead or alive. Will I be able to help them along their path?

The thought of only optical memories going through me, a conceived line of a sketch is incomprehensible. After searching for a mirror, and seeing the transformation is such an extension of the mind. Bending imagination. The sketch of the body's outer limits is a beautiful view, drawn with such practiced strokes. The details specialized, you can see attitude. A serious work of art. Inside this likeness is an observable progression with the freedom you allowed while living. The more natural and relaxed you are, the more intelligence materializes. This seems difficult, consenting to many elements, fact or fiction. If one sets a limit, then there is less to discover. Others' lives and their minds can draw attention, more art to see.

Grasping the new phase was a frightening penetration. An awakening of the spirits, amusing to them. To be, or not to be, on par with the dead. Despite having been told of the return to previous self, this stage contained qualities evident to others. Perceive the construction during this bare value. A true reveal, feelings and life on stage, the innermost secrets of a feature presentation. Not that many would have particular concern but having complete information of another, I could be uncomfortable with this. Would I discover any facts that could help uncover or introduce an exclusive item? Perhaps some distinct and limited facts as in hot information. Hot concerning a person's uniqueness, associated business, a connected link to a stolen article. My mind is racing, there would be a need to protect oneself and necessary to be very observant of others.

The arches and doorways of our Inn, however modest or well suited, are Spartan, simple and strong. There may seem grandeur, in comparison, with the marble and some aged carved arches. Shapes with communication through images.

Over the timeless years they have been the only vessels of travel, I think but know not. More conversations, seemingly casual, will help. Unofficial inquiries lay ahead and probable investigation. Training can open the eyes and mind. Here confrontation may be as simple as a question. You can see the truth. The competition could be the size of a memory, but you can double check with the moving photo albums. For the living this is no simple grocery list. Don't strain, retain. Give your head a shake and take it with you. Relax, life is a rough draft before achieving the past master.

The living once meeting any ghost, especially the one you are interested in, there is a complete alteration. What kind of reality is this? In which place, on earth as before, or somewhere on another level. Distinction is incomprehensible, perplexing beyond understanding. Is the body uncontrollable suspended in a moment of space and time. Are we vagabonds drifting while visiting a nameless nation? One can understand innumerable variations. Detached from the existing actuality, life as we know it. I am usually aware of the here and now, the improbable or unrealistic is fantasy for me. The only way to find out is to question. Do I have the brash to ask.

Stefani Pagliaro, our Italian artist comes across Vincent van Gogh, and no, she didn't have to wipe him off. Now chatting over a cheese plate and some red wine she learns of his Dutch heritage. She could see his livable surroundings, much art and dirty hands working hard. He was known for realism, post impressionism and modern art. He had hundreds of works in different materials but loved oil paintings. He sold only one in his life. He also had interests in gadgets and inventing. During their confident and appealing conversation he had been sketching her. Making smudges on his face as he pushed back his hair, oil paints were still covered but ready for action when he was. Getting to know each other's lives they walked into the dining room. A suffering thud came then a racing heart beating like the peak of cardio exercise so intense, your lungs feel as though they are not big enough to take in the breath you need. An unfamiliar feeling and perception lead to the throat like a painful aura. Almost the taste of death, a simple complex seizure before the appearance of her lovely outline. A constantly moving film of herself and family, the highlights running through her. You could see the care and realize the devotion of relationships. Also touch her personal style. She looked down at her body because Vincent's eyes were not on hers. The pictures progressing inside the sketch of her outline were worth seeing. He then had a strange pause, so she asked why. He plainly explained himself. He clearly thought he could have made a much better drawing of her. Stronger charcoal in some places and then not as dark, more delicate in others. It would also partner with her deft personality. He did not realize the bond between their interest was strong enough for him to take her to his next level. More actions and their description are available but let us leave room for arising circumstances.

Murray Silverstone had rounded the lounge to find Alexander the Great and shared some stories of adventure. He then stepped outside to have a look at the sky. I would prefer to question and know options before "living" it. Before I dive in, I need information above and beyond. Time to investigate and explore. On the ground and below give good clues but the Wright brothers saw more because they flew. From high in the sky the entire area does show what the average person could never know. Then see mostly clouds with a dark grey towards the east, spotted above with a lighter haze in the center. He was hoping for a clearing in the skies, then the orange and purple layers of sunset, like on the island of his ancestors'.

Diverse knowledge is preferred, here specifics perhaps a necessity. After bridging eight entryways, either in or out, those living become a permanent part of this phase. Most of the deceased have no need or wish to live again. You might be pessimistic and see yourself as trapped. You have been captured but this is no prison. With endless time you can research the history of people and the tactics of civilizations. Unforeseen studies of the future also await. Your memory may fall victim to capacity during these times. Be prepared for an infinity in your eighth arena. Interesting company and discovery await. Too few of the moments are sheer, timeless and pure. Will the dream keep us on the ground or are we somewhere else now that we've been found?

CHAPTER 5

DINNER WITH A DATE

Then recover and relish the Carnivore Café at 8: PM, if you can't tell the time, dress to the nines. Our menu is this evening's venue. Tonight, fashionably late is our permanent date. Your gut feeling will bring you. A whispering tummy can evolve to rolling echoes. You don't have to adore the antiquated décor. For most it is not out of date, matching so many, their fate. The latest here remember the memories, taste and feelings were created, images so true and clear. Without any fear of change. Would you prefer to die from, or for, the food on the menu? Age doesn't always work.... Arsenic and old lace might be good, in whipped cream if that's one of your themes. Now find a spot and be seated. If you say Sit and Shinola, you have a perfectly timed sense of humor.

The chiming of the clocks finally lowers the voices in the bar and on the terraces. The invitees regard each in the group their own way. They make a relaxed passage to the main dining hall. Where they are respectively announced upon entering. Prior to the introductions the Master of Ceremonies declared, "All should interact without intolerance. Despite the differences

97

of time frame, activities, surfaces and areas, passed on or still breathing. Let this party begin!" With some sophistication, glancing finds the seating arrangements, at the considerable number of round tables. Blended aromas drifted throughout the room, enticing nostrils and curious minds. The menus were firm linen certificates, selections engraved with bronze. Adonis was seated next to Al Capone. Cutlery and glasses of fitting shapes, four per person as beautifully laid as our guests. A silver lazy Susan was the center piece holding serving utensils and metal trivets. While being seated the head waiter at each table made remarks of hospitality knowledge, and their own welcoming comments. Henry the 8th was telling tales to Lady Godiva. After each course the centerpiece rotated, glasses were refreshed to match the fare, and guests moved one seat to the left. One visitor had been chosen and moderately removed for exclusive execution. For some it was torture, tantalizing only to the master. Disguised judges were making the rounds.

The dead acknowledged each other, each history was not only singular, but their activities were also matchless. They sauntered on and off the ground, greeting or eluding each other for various reasons. Going off the path for a moment. My history is unique yet unlike any song. From the time I was 20 until I was 40, physically there existed a distinct outline. I was so hot my bridesmaid was the city Fire Chief. Back on track. The dead were not devoted to one another. Some for very obvious reasons, J Edgar Hoover might have an Old Fashioned with the Pink Panther but may move on. Librarians could chat with blonde bombshells but eventually tidy up and put them on the shelves. Casually taking in the guests interface, their conduct and interaction.. Interest every moment, into your savings? Intrigue anticipated. I heard one sommelier mention while pouring red wine, "If there's something on your plate you don't recognize, introduce yourself." Ranjit Sing Maharaja was in a heated discussion with Buddha. One of the waiters in passing remarked, "If your hands get messy or sticky, whatever you do, lick them. Do not ask for finger bowls, this may cause unwelcome temptation from those attracted to digits." The judges smiled, nodding. Trying to relax while contemplating I decided it was best not to play with the food, it might fight back. Game may not be fare. The menu advised coffee and tea would be served in or outdoors, to individual preference. Spoons glittering under the moonlight reflecting off the shining, silver guillotine, would be a powerful sight. This after dinner mingling on the garden patio could be the beginning of the late-night endeavors. Thinking ahead, I stated, "If you feel the need to have me buried, remember my hormones and tastes will never die." The haunting will quickly begin, no matter what or how, I will not be forgotten. The end of this weekend is only the beginning. Next season, another event is being planned. Let's hope for a spring into summer. Why only kill time, when you can include others. Gambling for an invitation, shoot for the moon with your valor. There are a few here tonight. I hope it's in season, new guests and histories told. Dead or Alive? There's always a reward. Bon appetite. Now it's time for you to digest.

Our dinner choices at the Café where you can get everything from tenderloins to T-bone, from Chicago Black and

Blue to Crucified. Served on heated headstones, you can't beat our meat. Horseradish on the side giving tastebuds an extended sense. Our union rates for torture might be too costly for those that don't enjoy paying until you bleed. 'The Knife is my Wife", although still in the works is not ready for Broad Way. In progress we hope for "Still a Head", our crushing Wall Street mystery. Auditions for the Nashville rock and roll smash, "Hot Horse Radish", giving tastebuds a great whiplashing. The Big Way has nothing to lose once we crush it. Playing live the offers from Para Mountain will have to be treasure, once buried, twice alive. These projects are precious so don't wait to die, be trying. Underneath the BBQ sauce expect any number of surprises, from the unrecognizable to the undead. Scrape together what you can, get a good rate for the great escape. Winning prizes will be prosecco, red, white and champagne while dining. Slide into a nice wine, 99 is quite fine. Walter Cronkite is here to join and have a bite. If he likes it enough to rate us maybe he will write.

You'll find no rules on your plate, and only some meats cured.

Salads and cold dishes served on frost free platters for best taste and preservation.

To die for, Sushi and sashimi. Traditional style with riotous wasabi and ginger

Julius Caesar, the famous salad, or the cocktail, both delicious

Vincent Priceless caviar, toast points, sparse sprinkle of capers anoint.

Ceviche, scallops or large shrimp soaked in lime juice. It cooks in a marinade, a lot of citruses, a bit of olive oil and chopped cilantro. I like to add some grated ginger. Mix in a bowl gently with hands. No utensils mean no tears in the seafood. Leaving for two to four hours is sufficient. Served in a sleek wood bowl. The perfect partner is a Caesar cocktail, vodka based.

Poisonous Snakes; viper, asp, bitter once

Plato's Pizza, smallest feta squares tossed into ragu of sauteed cow brains. Tongue, liver, gizzards and other internal organs come from older recipes; we are happy to use them here. Crust dusted with pesto. We use after making only fresh ingredients. Unlike Plato, my brain is like the Bermuda Triangle, information goes in never to be found again.

Pirate's gold dusted fish and chips off the shoulder, rest in pieces. Two small oblong portions with crisps, not french fries

Friend or foie gras

Duck Soup is not a choice. A typical, but good portion, is what flies above and most of the population love. During this break in dinner, please refresh your glasses.

Enjoy some 1930s hilarity with Groucho, his wife's middle name. Also, Chico, Harpo and Zeppo. All these gentlemen were married several times. Is truth gentle, man?

Main Corpses: I cannot apologize for choices, dead or alive, dine at your own risk. Some of what the kitchen creates is the guests' guess.

If they could breathe, move and recreate. You might find them on your plate.

Dean Martin's Meatballs, choice of spaghetti or rigatoni and marinara sauce. Grated parmesan will top it all.

Adam's Rib Steak served by our chef, torched or blood-thirsty. Eve for dessert, a gastronomical flirt.

BBQ over white-hot coals Benjamin Franklin's sausage in a bun. Easy western fare.

An old favorite from overseas, Brains, black and bruised, served with pomegranate seeds with the choice of a side. Why be reserved?

Henny Youngman, one of the finest comedians with many memorable one liners, "Take my wife, please". I would too, but she's not on the menu. This may be more delectable than funny to the Cannibals in our crowd.

Another big ham on the menu, roasted with French Dijon mustard, ginger, squeezes of fresh lemon and a touch of brown sugar. Mix well and spread thickly. Extra ginger is nice. Just ask Gilligan.

Our Indian specialty, Curry That Can Be Furious. Choose one: red meat, chicken or seafood. Choice two: mild, medium or downright angry. Hit my hot spot please. Served with basmati rice and garlic naan bread. Ride the Orient Express. If you think you haven't been whipped enough, go to cooking school, here at the "Olde U".

Enjoy the house feature, our Man Eater's Fondue, do not worry it doesn't dine on you. Highly delicious and pretty tasty, especially for Femme Fatale. In bone broth, chicken reduction, shallots, garlic sliced, salt, pepper and oregano. John Dillinger chatted with Rosalind Russel. Don't forget a splash of french champagne, prohibition was no one's ambition.

Served fragrantly simmering, when the lid is removed the smell is to die for, take what you will from the guests' gold chests.

A mid spice devil brings the heat. Also, his fajitas, sizzling sufficiently, the cast iron serving dish flames and the smoke alarm goes off. The waitress squeezes half a lime over the inferno, trying to douse it and stop the show. No go. This amuses the diners so much there's a scattered loud applause. Any fires tonight? I'm no pyromaniac, just smokin'! A wafting grey cloud drifts lazily upward and the scent infuses my nostrils. No heat, just penetration. It's all good. Tonight, such a special delight.

Things become so tender they may fall in during this self-cooking dish and an unidentifiable morsel could appear, anywhere. Just say, Dr Livingstone I presume, between bites. Don't worry, you heel, if you'd like to dance you feel better. The accompanying condiments is an array of dips. Featuring the Enchanted Forest, Long Horn Ranch, Balsamic Volcano, Pureed Pig tails. Each one decadent and succulent..

Special of the Day – Seared Subordinates. This is our freshly fished course, as they were on Captain Bligh's ship. Tradition was with vintage metal weights, the finale. We sold out tonight. Originally sea water immersed, the salt-mine of preservation. The Irish pirate Anne Bonny's world is an oyster, enjoy the freshest snatch catch. Bring your camera and imagination if you'd rather snap chat.

Take a chance with two dies, ours are loaded. You may be too so let your life ride. Don't try the hard ate. For your pleasure choices are thrashed potatoes, in the center ring creamed corn, plucked, then sliced tomatoes or green has beans. Unreasonably influenced. Let us stand to remember a friend's effort. Over three thousand years our food inspector has dragged his sorry tastebuds and butt. So many cuisines from different parts of the universal tongue and tummy, then the sum, regarding uncountable ptomaine intoxications. All have brought our man through sixteen phases of culinary casualties. We thank you, very much. You're humble and amuse us.

Veg of the day, wild rice, roasted roots, Skullcap Mushrooms, Rhubarb Leaves, Suffering Succotash, Mashed potatoes in grave E, Poppy's Heroine Salad, sharply garnished with diamond shards. Romaine and Cannabis salad served by the eighteenth century South American police, Spicy Fish Eyeballs, each intended breath brings pungent death, and finally Heel and toes undressed. In moonshine, impressed? Our culinary care, the tantalizing tips can bare, accompanied by selection of dips. Careful when thirsty, the water, really everything is infectious. All enjoyed it better under dressed.

Use precaution while dining. Eat and drink slowly to savor every bite, you may enjoy someone else's lips. Don't plan to choke yourself down.

All dishes particularly good with house red wine, Chateau Zero. Our compliments to you. The only whining here will be prosecco, white, champagne and port. The clinking of glasses after a toast brings a hollow sound even when ¾ full. Following a sip, watching the ghostly guests, see the liquid sink down the throat. And what's a spread without freshly dead, or homemade bread... let me know when you knead it. Those dining close to the open leaded glass doors or on the starlit terrace enjoy your dinner. If any pollen comes to rest on your food that's natural. Any ashes that pass by or land on your chosen dishes I will give two observations. First there is a breeze, most can shoot it, but few can stop it. Then secondly some undead have not crossed the final process. There is a fine line between them. Enjoy what's coming, tonight and in your own existence. No matter what the busy night plans we'll try our best not to stall service, our waiters are eager to please. It deserves it and defines it. Though our guest are timeless, at some point we'll all exit, stage left.

Our finales include fresh desserts Lawrence of Arabia's recipe, Crème de Camel, two humped I believe. Our fruit is so fresh, once you pierce the skin, the innocent flavor is like a tidal wave on the tongue. Traditional Jelly Roll, a southern cake with jam. Interesting information on the name so let's dish the dirt on this dessert. Ferdinand Joseph Lamont born in New Orleans 1890 became a pianist, a ragtime bandleader then later composer of jazz orchestrations. Known as Jelly Roll Morton during his hay daze. Not only his music deep and rhythmical, but laughter also rang out from his heart in every song. Songs and compilations, 38 in total include King Porter Stomp, Original Jelly Roll Blues and Dead Man Blues. A life so full, in 1939 after being stabbed twice at the Jungle Café in Washington, he died later in 1941. Such creative sound, artistic and inspirational and a love life well rounded. His intimate passion and personal currant became a pun related to local gossip. These attributes are well known for his taste. The term jelly roll intimated physical femininity, juicy and smooth, shapes correlated creating a surrounding. You could only surrender completely. Getting down to it, after time this expression became a synonym for an orgasm. Morton's stylish rage, trends by choice, a sophisticated exaltation, now a vintage memory. In the record of jazz these words of pleasure, and related thoughts will always come. Never exhaust the treasures of life, appetizing treats. Whet your lips and put them here.

Capella can be quite pleasing but is not yet on the list, no cutlery necessary.

Simple fruit, the grapes of wrath. Succulent madness.

Quicksand pie, a la strode, no chance to scream. There's no bluff, you'll be engulfed.

Spice cake with red devil icing, more than a piquant piece. Wear your horns and be naughty. Brought by your maid, a personal touch in your chamber, as it is take-out only.

With coffee and liqueur or cognac Benjamin Franklin raises his glass to say, "Moderation could be the father of procrastination."

Some of our more prominent guests, and those perhaps with underlying reasons, had protectors of many kinds. Some surveyors went to check the food, others kept up with news and the currents of the gathered people. One can never be too sure, or comfortable, without backup. Support through time has rarely been without extortion. Some go forward without looking behind. If only it was that easy.

At this event and feast you can reminisce, over the years, about Being Taken Out. Guests at Dinner With the Dead include Alphonse Gabriel Capone, infamous for racketeering and murder, who can forget the taking out on Saint Valentine's... a massacre. Add prostitution and cashing in on moonshine during prohibition. John Dillinger's rampage during nineteen thirty-three and nineteen forty-four included thievery, killing 10 men, wounding others and dispatching a sheriff. Baby Face Nelson started robbing banks April 1st 1930 and took out rival men with violence from his temper. Sadistically. These men were endangered by a takeout service, no food, just the deduction of money. Having many competitors and fighting any edit.

Some of our visitors have unquenchable appetites and questionable lives, loved or not, come with their staff only. After several courses and seating changes the rearrangement brought Groucho Marx next to Don Rickles. Not only decades separated their popularity but also the approach to humor. Add Don's natural, forthright and sarcastic manner. You may think that Marx's sexually suggestive jokes were ahead of the early 1900s, along with their attacks on high society. Don Rickles was right in your face and left no stone or personal trait unturned. What interesting characters as table mates. It was the first meeting, so they eagerly chatted about vaudeville, Broadway, comedy clubs and TV. There was easy, natural laughter between them. Don was reminiscing about some earlier days and told this story. "When I was a young man in high school, I had a job at the ice cream counter in the Pharmacy. I thought it first class as there were about 6 seats in front and with quite the selection to choose from and had customers often. One afternoon the door opened slowly, and a gentleman entered. Looking left then right he slowly came towards my counter. His stiff walking was most awkward, but he kept on. Choosing a seat, he sat down quite cautiously as I greeted him. Well good sir, what will it be today? I have chocolate, fresh strawberry and vanilla. With a glimmer of anticipation and desire, he licked his lips and asked for strawberry. I decided on a bowl and started doing my thing. He shifted himself once. I was generous with 2 scoops. "Would you like whipped cream," he nodded eagerly. I placed a napkin and spoon out for him as I asked if he liked the dripping of chocolate sauce. As he eased himself again, his strained but charming smile had a hint of wickedness, so I poured it lightly in a circle. Crushed nuts I asked?" "No," he replied, "arthritis."

Time to comment on, an alternative parallel, Juan Mayal Diala discovered three islands and named them El Carteses. From this the name Al Catraz was developed. Juan was roughly 200 years younger than that location, so it was not on his list of seasonal vacations. Men who tell tails you may find in jail, was one of his reminders. At the saloon, wanting a snack he orders ceviche, a rare seafood delight. To drink, not necessarily in this order, a friend El Patron, a shot of tequila and a margarita on the rocks. Rocks, I'm not referring to his beaching your boat. The beverages arrive first, and he sets in to enjoy his first sips. At the table he takes the seat next to Marilyn Monroe. This evening they expected to watch an unusual show. Each guest was partaking. Some giggled, others just pickled. As many people do his eyes openly gazed on her breast area rather than her body, bedlam. He should have been focused inside the sketch of her body, a running display, the best spectacle in town. Her facts and life, needing not to ask her to reveal any assets. She ordered a glass of champagne and snackwich, ham with Dijon and ginger. While they become acquainted, during their drinks the food arrives. This evening one should expect nothing but the unique. Looking at the thermometer, go hot, not only your dog. Don't mistake it for a Temperance Lecture, that's cold turkey. And the middle of the road could be tres risqué. The plates were small electrum discs ancient men used as safeguard when fighting. The cutlery on the table was old as the first forged alloy. The napkins were cut from the medieval cloth worn under mesh tunics for man at arms. History is not a side, yet they looked at their dinner. The nice thick slice of

steaming ham not only had the fragrance of the marinade, but
it also had a snout. To the guests' curious eyes it seemed not
snuffling. Great for Juan, he could smell the lemon more than
the cilantro on the ceviche, a true cooking marinade, but the
tentacles of the squid were waving in time to Sinatra's Love and
Marriage. Well, they had nothing to lose, time to graze. When
next to Marilyn it is not rare to stare. All celebrities appreciate this, it's something easy to become used to. Regardless of
the uniqueness of the saloon and restaurant all drinks and food
were meant for a king. Leader of the pack.

It was dessert for the feast. Not far, nor flashy just distinguished, Stella engraved in gold above the door. One of the
room doors draped with heavy velvet black. Long to the floor,
like a living room set. Placed fairly close to the dining hall. To
one person's knowledge it had a very low bed with two thin
iron posts adjacent. There was another closed door almost
camouflaged on one of the inner sides of the room. On the
opposite wall there was a very large piece of metal forming
the letter C. There was a hinge so it seemed it could be moved
out from the wall while still attached. One thinks perhaps a
safe or treasure is behind. What wonder of unknown pleasurable pain came between these walls. They were flat and
had the smoothness of a dry skinned pelt. The metal on the
wall was surprisingly room temperature while the square iron
posts were almost cold to the touch. The base of the low bed
had thick wire rings where each post met, also halfway up
them. There was large smooth rope piled into rings, landing
in circular piles on the floor. The closed inside door was as

unmenacing as a closet. Until a person was selected and led there by one of the judges. Patiently waiting was a beautiful woman with jet black hair, in high heeled boots that fit snuggly up to her thighs, wearing soft darkest lamb skin clothes, close to her figure. Stella was the mistress and ruling resident. She attended those lured or sent to her. There was also a wide leather belt on her waist, nowhere close to evil. It was succulently soft, even sensual to the touch. Farther and further, hung on a hook, which was the same colour of the door so almost invisible, there was a smooth long object. To the common eye it looked like a wand. Quite thin, and barely bendable, so more like a fairy's or witches'. What the door, (like a classy closet), enclosed was a secret at this point. Anticipation was not necessarily intended, and never shown in any way. After a kind question, a blindfold placed securely would avoid any useless, conversation. Foreshadowing would be instantaneous for many. Weakness gave inquisitive ideas, of timing and the treatments. At leisure Stella cleaned utensils to shine, hard or soft, a daily and enjoyable duty. Trying them for precision, swoosh, snap! Some of her essentials, she used oils to renew surfaces, in preparation. Being both cautious and precise, wisely she lubricates them with potions from pufferfish, fire ants, virus carrying mosquitos, to snake poison. Not far from those ingredients, the mixing station provided the makings of a dry and dirty martini, her favorite personal poison. There was sunken lighting and speakers to gently provide endless and repeated sound effects, motion and also music. Currently low blues was playing, then after she took a long sip, sanding softly echoed. A light pounding then a snap was reasonably low key in the background. You could hear her soft breathing coming closer.

Samantha Yardley has found her place card, an inviting seat, next to William Shakespeare. She finds him old-fashioned, shy and conscientiously quiet. She introduces herself as he looks toward her. With her shiny, natural cranberry lips, she explains her life's fascination in literature and training. Mentioning her interest, being specifically drawn to his work. "You know of it?" was his reply. She remarked on how she and, "Others have studied your words, which for generations have been admired. They have been republished multiple times, acted in plays, movies and highly respected." After his quizzical expression regarding movies he looks her over a second time. He gets in one statement. "I've heard of and seen little in my realm." But enthralled she continues, "Your work is regarded as incomparable." She asked about his death. "In history, April 23rd 1616, it's been known as his falling ill after a night of drinking. Legend has it, although this exact time is unknown, it was supposed he and two writers, Ben Johnson and Michael Drayton, were out celebrating." William came forth with one of his quotes, "Cowards die many times before their deaths". Their chatting and related easy laughter was slowly interrupted by the waiter, an actor working for cash tips while he waited for a role. He smiled politely and licked the tip of his pencil, "Have you decided on dinner this evening?" Executing his image of an efficient head waiter, also playing his part of the evening, Samantha smiled and nodded. "Is the

Special ready because I am too." In her now husky voice she ordered, "A Caesar salad, hold the senate members, followed by Dean Martin's Meatballs, with Penne, please." Finished she regarded Shakespeare. As he ordered the curry with a mite of spice, Samantha suggested they could share the salad she ordered. He looked hesitant as he spoke, "My pleasure, are you sure?" She shone, nodding her consent. It was her desire and inclination. Top of the list, the first line in her mind's eye.

Differences create meanings and beauty. The Chateau Zero was poured into the empty decanter, and smiling, Will gave them each a portion in their goblets. "If this is early," smiling he asked with style, "we usually let it breathe a while." Samantha was in admiration of him as a historic writer and as a man. Shameless, through and through, she conjectured dessert, champagne and lush fruit. She explained further the study of his sonnets and plays in total. How they have been placed as Comedies, Tragedies and History. 4 poems and an illustrious Collection of Sonnets first published in 1609. In a live conversation hearing the history after his death, from a lively young lady, was a new experience. If she was a little fresh, he was bound to blush. She was a special learned scholar of literature. Also, easy to look at, an enjoyable encounter overall. The wine and salad started off a good meal, very tasty with a squeeze of lemon. The bug on the fresh lettuce was garden variety, after eating it he just threw the leaf on the ground. A common practice in the pubs he frequented. As her eyes opened wide, he laughed and said it was too big to be a cockroach. Having no fear of moon flower, especially the seeds, he gathered plant-based poison.

Some critics need not judge. He had no arm for aiming but very good for writing. A patient, tortured brain must go with that. A lot of hard labor, looking over stolen blank pages. He speculated many nights, trying to find the right words, laboring with blood, sweat and ink. And that's no whine, if he only had the chinks to pay. A B C D E, Flog the G, With a beaker or two I will forge past where, X Y and Z fell. Hopefully not down the well, but wines cab get twisted. When life gets busy, and there are always times, stalling is not necessarily the best answer. Pausing for another thousand years? We are already suspended, now let's play! As long as there are stars in the sky who would ever know or ask us why? There will be plenty of time toward being at rest. There is no harm in entertaining.

At my liberty I'll share information regarding gratuities. For those who serve, please be generous when deserved. After cocktails at the Spirits' In, I offered the attendant a cash bonus for efficient service, the amount mindfully liberal. With respect, handing the tray with the bill, and courtesy payment. Afterwards, with an almost sinister grin, he abusively replied, "Thank you kind madame but I've seen bigger tips in diapers." His smirk turned into a big smile with the broadest clear dark green eyes. I could not help but laugh with him. Beaming, I spoke about my line of work and replied, "diamonds are usually mine." He thought to himself, my collection of beautifully moisturized leather whips work with any collection of finery. The days of leather and lace…

TOMB SERVICE

Be careful with your alarm clock, it has two features, a sleep timer and one of the options is erase. You don't want to miss a thing.

For Breakfast, please indicate personal choices on your request sheet. Chef's suggestions:

Eggs come first at the Inn, as the chicken has crossed the road, and you can choose a side. Cooked to order, toast with jam, a classic alarm. Eggs freshly laid, like some current guests. Fresh is only a speculation. Meats: bacon or peameal, request crisp or juicy, and sausage patties. Tenderloin steak is available. Selections are well done, mediocre and a few prefer "take its horns off and wipe its ass" rare. Toast varieties are Mediterranean white, Prairie whole wheat, for most European dark pumpernickel or rye with caraway seeds. Juices, freshly squeezing our annoying prep manager, are orange, crispy sour, sweet apple, pure pomegranate and the ripest tomato. Plates garnished with fresh veg, fruit or both, as your choice. Our French pressed coffee is Columbian, Fair Trade, served hot. Preferred options of cream or milk, and side of white sugar or Caribbean cane granules. From the equator, feel yourself there, just stir it up. Enchanting energy from the scullery.

Shall we get to the chasing of blues away. I have previously mentioned some wake me up syrups. Alternate beverages, branded as rejuvenation Spirits, are well known at the Inn. Champagne and OJ, wanted as number one, for so long. The quenching Prosecco with cranberry and pure pomegranate juices, a combination of sweet, an unassuming pucker, delicious and slightly effervescent. The Bloody Mary, spiced with pepper sauce, unusual with horseradish, no harry caray. A popular modern tradition, the Caesar. Originally from Calgary, ride the cowboy and not the horse! With your preferred selection of vodka, sensations from global nations. Rim the glass with celery salt, add Clamato juice, hot spice and a stalk of celery. A slice of citrus tops the glass, squeeze into the drink and it balances the flavors. If you are really hung over, a Tequila Seizure is my advice. With a lime slice wet the rim, spice it up traditionally with celery salt. After the ice, tequila, if you want a change try Montreal Steak Spice or go to Mexico with a mixture of chili powder, dehydrated lime, fresh ground pepper and salt. Nothing up my sleeve, just a few years and natural flair, pretty but not fair. Garnish with a blanched jumbo prawn, spicy pickled green beans or just blanched, firm asparagus. Additional options are a skewer of Greek kalamata olives, pickled onion, green olives with pimento, even anchovies. Go to town with what you like, imagination has no limit. Spice this drink first with 2 dashes of preferred hot sauce, 3 drops Worcestershire, squeeze ½ lime, be as fresh as you can. There are those that like it quite hot, but this is one cool drink. Giddy-up and go! When spicey, the whip comes out, but no cream.

Other mains; Eggs Benedict Arnold with smoking hash browns

Cream of wheat, made by old mother Macdonald, the real McCoy. Molasses or maple syrup with fruit on the side, our fruit is always fresh… watch out for that pinch!

As previously mentioned, to wake up, a spicy Bloody Mary with her double barrel shot. A morning quencher, wild and will smooth the evening's clench. Worchester stirs you from sleep, shake away those counted sheep.

Fresh OJ, not Simpson but deadly delicious

Fair Trade coffee, a dark horse from the tropics, bet the long shot. Anthony Bourdain, a food critic, has not joined our party yet or dined. He had no invitation, but traditionally, that's never stopped him before. Cusumano Nero D'Avolo, another worthy wine. Famous chef Georges Auguste Escoffier became known as the king of chefs, and the chef of kings. Born Oct 28, 1846, in Villeneuve France until his passing February 12, 1935, in Monte Carlo. During his life he was a French commis chef, restaurateur, and culinary writer updating and popularizing cooking methods. He was director of the kitchen, chef de cuisine, both at the Savoy Hotel and the Carlton Hotels in London. An exceptional life and superior career.

Once you are refreshed and ready for more, today's activities are yours. Introductions by chance, for meetings relaxed. In the saloon, people mix near the bar, flow and mingle near or far. Sharing chronicles by choice, maharaja or maid, voice your recognizable behavior. Authentic in your white Grecian kilt or sarong of the serious Mayans. Atop their pyramid is a smaller hollow structure. Here shown heroic placements of beautiful, priceless gems inside the small stone den topping the pyramid. See the striking emerald in the darkest part. My attention your philosophies, Plato. They built the first institution of higher learning during the Athenian classical period;

The Academy of Thought. Keep chilling and open seamlessly allowing steps forward. Time to shine while you dine, make new friends, take pleasure in a good meal and stay. Jules Verne can spin a great yarn along with other guests. We can set ourselves free and learn about each eternity. If any of the guests wants to bet me ten dollars, I am dead, I'd be afraid to take it. Who knows what will happen?

Of all the institutions and every book you pass through, take another look. Stop reigning in and just let go, feel free and let yourself grow. Imagination is everything, an assorted preview of life. Each breath you take, and every step is natural. Until a stopped flow. All the lights are synchronized, look for green, initiation takes off. The places you have been, and every person you have met seem authentic and accurate, your school of life. These were learning tools so simple and sincere. What makes you smile on this personal road may later help you to cry and lessen an overload. Reading while sunbathing may make you well red. Let your thoughts be free as you allow life's release. You cannot apologize for early years and errors, some choices were not premeditated. Life is unpredictable while Death is unavoidable so do not be afraid of this category. What is in between birth and your anxiety of death can be much worse. Avoid the red lights enroute, see inviting warm cinders, be careful of your fingers. Beware of this path as you walk and leisurely talk, as it bends. Just breathe, exercise movement, interact and communicate. If you can, this is life's clock. Shoulders back and down, tense your belly. One thought may be to have control, but time is just an unassuming stroll. Difficulty will rear its ugly head; you may think you are ready and not yet dead. Hold on if you are able. Just try to manage what is possible, monitor what you can, this may be your limit. Life can be complicated so go to your past and remember this is the school of your life. This contract you had with the world once you left is what tied you up. The innocence of birth gives you a blank slate, to have your thoughts and hope for the best. It is possible that an act will restrict in spite of management. In a reasonable world negative and positive should balance. Regardless of what you have been taught, there is no limit to the freedom of any thought. If an electrical device can be a circuit breaker for the direction of pain, this requires expertise. To devise and then release it. You may have grasped this along your way, or been left to its restriction, without control stray. This menace can bind and bring agony, while the process of consciousness can influence the limit you can hold. Willpower is there, can one discipline events in every whisp of air. Unimaginable. That is a complexity beyond command. When we come to this with organization, always an unanswered question remains. Sometimes there is no gain. Opportunity can come by chance, changing direction. What comes next?

What seems wrong is a dark place we have never been. The impression of right has the lighter side we have seen. Some life still will be lit, something we can look forward to. This is the road we are on, though unfinished, we maneuver. Think like Plato just slip and let fly the restraints of daily norm, your brain won't die, there is more to form. Let existing trials bring energy that helps you grow. This is true learning, some mistakes could recycle. We should endure and survive what is real, here and now. Recollections, some fond, a few unkind, others may be sudden and objectional. A natural response may have a smile, then heart and mind stand away, there are screams from behind. All judgement leave in the obscurities, they will be not only seen by others but mostly felt again. Remember this may not be the end. The past, and just the memories, summon up the dreams and actions of life. They can interact with you now, a whisper in the shadows or a shriek in the back street. Unexpected obstruction comes, and with frustration prevents the clarity of knowledge. There's no turning the clock, though directions replaced, now your head's on the block. We come from the enclosed warmth of our mother. Then coming into the light, this cold difference, in that instant we naturally have fright. Cry out for the startling changes. After a life of many, there's more to come, some completely stranger. While we are connected and warm, are there any faults? Does this in reverse replicate death? I think the benefits of sunshine, like the dimming of evening, give joy. Very cold seasons kill most life forms. Many give oxygen, food and warmth, the needs to survive. So energizing and nourishing is daybreak, a balmy relaxed afternoon, then followed by a beautiful sunset. I felt life was better than the alternative. Some grave work to get back there. What occurred was live, but I left more than half behind. Best to feel this surface, stage and level of knowledge. Let it take you and show how to heal what you can, few can stop it. What's behind is the ease and emotion, now blacked out confusion, what comes next? Learn to appreciate your mind, this point is the time. There is a need to develop and improve, evolution to succeed, happiness advances. Ahead of time, why leave what was behind. One can amend, try and remember before the end. Is there really one? We cannot see who or what's in the lead. Keep your head, Dine with the dead.

Costume jewelry? I think not, we'll be on a string to the stars. Our late afternoon, evening event... the required attire calls for your natural taste or imagination. In sixty-nine BC Cleopatra had a private team to help her dress. Trained in decoration and arrangement of face painting, then the placement of silk panels for robes. To achieve the desired result is an art, knowing her physical being is most important. There are people in modern times who have surpassed others with genuine talent in these areas. Here we have instinctive and versatile skills with brilliant results. In art and sculpture the strong, smooth curves of Michael Angelo to the cubism paintings of Pablo Picasso. Painters Edward Degas and Vincent van Gogh. Vincent went into a rage with Pablo and cut off his right earlobe. Afterward he gave it to a prostitute, such a gift could cause a less desirable position to fill. There are more interesting activities I hear in passing, to incite and achieve.

In the art of personal preparation let us go from the inside out. After eating fresh foods for health and taking vitamins, relax and meet William Tuttle, makeup artist. He has worked with many women and men, actors, some a beautiful backdrop. And energizing, while others a challenge, anything but easy. Both types include some adornment with cosmetics, or times adding pieces to fashion, a period in history. Seeing this gift is knowing his genius. Sydney Guilaroff can take your hair anywhere. Born in 1907, England, his hairdressing reflected centuries past and modern highlights from 1934 until the late 1960s. A crowning glory of vintage images. He'd be the first to say better to be dyed than here today. Let us get dressed. Ellen Tracy toiled using research and an enthusiastic edge, a limitless verge without boundary. To have the luck of transportation by the natural success of her individuality. Impressions completed by investigative education, her accomplishments, and the realization of selection. In countless ways she is the best choice. To have costume designed and fitted by this woman and her team, is complete authenticity and originality, giving an exhilaration. Her results show years of resource, expertise and tacit talent. Encompassing finest ability, an unblocked quality. With this crew these people can outfit you to desire. Historical or current, you will express, in some dashing form of dress. For this gala celebration, anything goes!

Attire and costumes; Adam and Eve, we have mentioned their fall leaves, and seasonal grapes will be casual and wear their genes. At dinner this evening refrain from saying "pass the figs please". The Devil and Red Skelton, the colors easily exchanged, and personalities at times are a joke. Ella Fitzgerald's voice flies like the wings of a morning dove. Jesus of Nazareth, with soft heart and mind bright as the sun, a lord's history at large. The Rat Pack, rodents with ice-colored jackets, music just as cool. Einstein never a square, cherry pie, very round. Cleopatra and Liz Taylor, both a canvass waiting to be painted, easy for William Tuttle. Mary Magdalen and Mother Teresa can donate silken robes for the poor and find Ellen Tracy. The Marx Brothers are typically odd a perfect switch for brothers in the 'hood. Marylin Monroe in Some Like it Hot, dressed by Orry-Kelly. One could never forget the small gems on the flesh toned gown, just obscuring feminine truths. Directions of a sleuth. She had such sparkle, a diamond in the rough. Elvis almost never changes his studded or jeweled suit, just those blue, blue, Blue Suede Shoes. Liberace, on his grand piano in a mountain of color and gems, put on those ruby slippers too. A recent president, of questionable character in an orange clown suit, trying to get out of a strait jacket. Aquarius comes as an emerald mermaid with porpoise. Don Rickles wears a big smile as insults come as hysterical humor. Hostess at the Cafe, one broiling hot chick, comes in a riverboat steaming along in an apron. Pepe le Pew poses with his striped tail upwards, his smile holding a rose. Bugs Bunny comes as Dr. Edward Jenner who developed injectables. Is that why the duck is daffy? Tarzan comes with Jane, their fig leaves dressed as animal skins. Shakespeare pierces us with words. Most females in history grace us, including Cleopatra, Nefertiti, and the legendary Aphrodite goddess of sex. Her dress is nothing at all, significantly revealing. Now that is fitting.

John Wayne, our cowboy of honor is dry as a gourd, so bartender, with haste, please have some whiskey poured. Leave the bottle and with tradition a few more glasses. He must have more friends, besides his horse, always a beautiful Bay. Customarily a quiet man, he quotes, conversation is an illusion, it is just a long monologue. WC Fields never gave a sucker an even break, including his wife, the old bat. People of various ages can recall Bela Lugosi portraying Count Dracula in 1931. The Count was a Transylvanian from the family of Atilla the Hun. Pennsylvania 6, 5000 could not be the number of victims whose blood was drank. Why not have the cocktail du Jour in our lounge, the Mace Martini. Garnished with a historical spiked, metalhead, the records show customs and visualization. The ceremonial staff we use as a model for a cocktail skewer through cloves of garlic. Best for masking the smell of the chemical usually sprayed from this weapon. Only a strong, valiant scent that accompanies a cocktail when in close range will do.

During the twentieth century smoking cigarettes was a popular part of life. Mostly while socializing during cocktail and entertainment hours. We could light them with Hercules' symbol, a lightning bolt, to start the party. It was such a custom of many occasions people held or had cases filled, to provide them, a popular custom. Sharing these white cylinders of dried tobacco leaves involved offering them from silver square containers that clicked open. There were coffers, upon coffee tables, made from many substances. Nineteen-nineteen to nineteen thirty-nine, Art Deco glass and gold, very chic, designs unparalleled. Bakelite in the thirties was in. It could be opaque, translucent or even transparent. A material with the eye-catching beauty of a gem. It was made from a byproduct of the blending of phenol and formaldehyde. Some under running hot water gave the smell of acid. Smoking produces ashes, as cigars, cigarettes or pipe tobacco is burned. So, ash trays, shaped circular, in a rectangle or imaginative shapes were readily placed. Glass, metal or ceramic were the popular substances. Outdoors, ashes can travel in the breeze, while some just shoot it. Some may complain about this dust, but many enjoy a good blow. A typhoon or gale have also been weathered. Gale being from the Norse word Gallen meaning mad, frantic or enchanted. Like a girls' night out! Alcohol can cause inebriation while grapes surely enamor the tongue and palate.

I believe enjoyment with reservation is the way to book a table. Use these weapons dressed for dinner at eight. These fermented beverages became restricted completely. Prohibition outlawed the manufacture, sale and transportation in the United States from Jan seventeen, nineteen-twenty, to Dec fifth, nineteen-thirty-three. Too long. The mafia and crime bosses were the runners of guns, gambling and alcohol, routinely known as booze. Powers of influence gainfully $ought. For thirteen years the cost was high, but the goods were rare and captivating. Very often bought for personal or professional reasons. Without the shadow of a doubt, we each have a horse of a different color.

CHAPTER 6

THE SEVEN PERCENT SOLUTION

After the weekend of events both old and new, the near and far-out, let's use a cliché from the stories of Sherlock Holmes. Also, in nineteen fifty-four meaning excellent or wonderful, originally in jazz talk. It seems now is a good time for some of the solution, the historical mainline. Afterward it might bring some misapprehension. You won't be deluded. But never on this day, what you have seen is what you get. Here is the overall conclusion. The great halls of the Inn were alive with the melody and orchestra, of all time, in chord. I had been thrilled and could only grant them the floor. The rock of ages were several things. The marvelous and sleek marble, the magnificence of the granite in the grand gardens. A suitable setting for our guest's profound, intense and abundant spirits. No pint intended. Dinner, an occasion in full swing with music, beverages and tastes from the globe. Chef Georges Auguste Escoffier shared himself saying he did not come for the food, he arrived for the company. The multiple courses had been the mingling, beverages, dinner and dancing. Breakfast fit for a king, are they right and which one's still left. Who's along for the ride, escorting the living in and out of the phases of total existence. Life is just a little in the middle. From the known beginning of our planet, world and ancient organized society, the Roman empire and the importance of philosophy evolved. From the Mediterranean to the European Middle Ages, through to the more recent days of North America. The significant moments of heritage were relived in their days and ways, verifiable. Chronicled by expert archivists while guests travelled in times of their choice. With little conceal-ment there was consent to coincide and favourably harmo-nize. The scant cloaking was easily ignored with so much to amaze, learn, view and adore. Drawing attention were Michael Angelo, Rafael and Da Vinci while the poets made remarkable notes. Men and women of science compared per-sonal findings as intellectuals studied consequential minds. Historians wrote while the actors joked and in westerns drew their guns. Historical heartthrobs swallowed beer watching others sip cheerfully. Millennial inspiration from the trials of nations. Shared enlightenment by Einstein and Socrates, their minds are diamonds not in the rough. A memorable gathering, wonder satisfied, yet some judgements tried. The evening enjoyed, slave next to the King while Ella and Sinatra sing. The waltz romanced the Charleston, the jive was twisted next. A feast with the passed and the four alive minds may there be other times. Imagination can extend several kinds. Samantha Yardley leaves to allow Shakespeare to go on as he will, writing the words of life. Not just finished, let's say the finest. She does leave with the one last word, en francais, Fine.

Think of a reason for another season. Another time with interest inclined. Autum orchards, fields ripe, vines bowing with full grapes. Now the apples from the tree, a ripe color and firm, picked for a juicy crunch. Each bite, as chewed, a part of life comes alive. Pears in an early frost, a large portion forever lost. The vines holding grapes too long, those newer and soft are best harvested for wines better with a bit of acidity. The vines bring some of the boldest wines. Mature, robust and befitting, ready to drink. There are a few not fit to drink, nor are they worth the ink. If the apple has a worm, then it's a table for two. Delicious, ripe raspberries, watch out for the red juice, like blood, dripping from your fingers. Try the fruits of the earth as you go, the bounty fills all senses. Feel your food, touch and see, look for the best. Avoid disappointments especially twenty-year sentences. Hear the crunch of the carrot, the first pop of the grape as its juice floods the mouth, teasing, then pleasing the tongue. Tantalized by the smell of juice from a watermelon as it's sliced, the cutting board runneth over. Seet or sour, now might be the hour. Taste is a mouth reborn. Naughty or nice will you be chosen twice? Our beautiful garnish, rose petals, watch out for the thorns, as you pick you can get pricked. The sun, so tired of lifting its bright head, lay lazily, drifting just below the horizon. Like an overworked well looking for a new source in an aging bay, sucking the earth for its life. On this occasion it is time to choose, dead or alive will you win or lose. No matter it's been first rate! The place, sensations and tastes, present and past will make us whole. The entire being, able to live a full life, now and ever after.

Now I leave you with a poem.

LIVING THE DREAM

With the brilliant cry of their outer show the stars lit up the skies

Feel related chemistry, enjoy who arrive and their mysteries

Slowly savour the night as much as the delicious food.

The endless are boisterous at this gala, death had a ball

Time's influence, music, and intrigue make the mood.

Remember all lives never die, please pick up this call

Inspired artists genuinely drew as the four winds gently blue.

All existed now and then, invited to the drawing room or den

The evening wore on, introductions then acquaintance-ship came often

Don't worry or pause, moving tales have happy endings

Their unique impressions give new sensations

Features of your life, the portrait's not yet done

Years have been given; I hope you paid attention

Now it's time to learn what we will eventually earn

Allow feelings while alive, give life all you can

Continue fundamentals nourishing all functions

Maintain, even amplify, life and death are a junction

Experience's influence is truth and timeless

Best to imagine and think, your history will be a link

How far is forever, there will always be more

Dine with the dead, through infinite doors

Let intrigue captivate and walk with thought

No one had to say goodbye, the dinner was to die for.

Words on these pages have been thought, put together and now I guess my head's been read. Pease take my thoughts with you to bed.

As dinner winds down and people raise glasses a question is pondered. Who came first and which will last? They can only wonder and may care for another glass. It is getting late so let's check out our rooms. I'll put on my nightcap, and we can have a private sip. Then see you, after breakfasting in bed, at the mourning. When you tell my story do not give it an ending. Just blow out the light.

Here's to you and have a Very Good Knight.